C000072370

PENGUIN

THE NIGHT O

Kayce Teo, who writes under the pen name Leslie W, was one of six mentees selected for the Mentor Access Project's Fiction category, an annual programme by the National Arts Council, Singapore, which develops young and emerging writers in Singapore's four official languages. This book was written under the mentorship of the prolific local writer, Dave Chua. Kayce worked as a journalist in Singapore Press Holdings' magazines arm, and is currently the regional editor at TheSmartLocal.com, one of Singapore's top lifestyle portal. Two of her short stories were published in an anthology Pulp Toast / Roti Bakar.

The Night of Legends

Leslie W.

PENGUIN BOOKS

An imprint of Penguin Random House

PENGUIN BOOKS

USA | Canada | UK | Ireland | Australia
New Zealand | India | South Africa | China | Southeast Asia

Penguin Books is part of the Penguin Random House group of companies
whose addresses can be found at global.penguinrandomhouse.com

Published by Penguin Random House SEA Pte Ltd
9, Changi South Street 3, Level 08-01,
Singapore 486361

Penguin
Random House
SEA

First published in Penguin Books by Penguin Random House SEA 2019

Copyright © Kayce Teo

10 9 8 7 6 5 4 3 2 1

This is a work of fiction. Names, characters, places and incidents are either the
product of the author's imagination or are used fictitiously and any resemblance
to any actual person, living or dead, events or locales is entirely coincidental.

ISBN 9789814867979

Typeset in Adobe Caslon Pro by Manipal Technologies Limited, Manipal
Printed at Markono Print Media Pte Ltd, Singapore

www.penguin.sg

To Mama,
I miss you every day.

1

Reawakening

A girl floated, weightless in the cold, silvery water. Her long, jet-black hair drifted, tenderly caressing cheeks sunken from malnutrition like a bibliophile's fingertips skimming over aged books. With her back straight and hands clasped to her chest, she was a vision of peace. A snaking cable as thick as her waist coiled around her waiflike body to form a black cocoon, giving her an additional layer of concealment within the watery depths in which she was suspended.

Her eyelids fluttered. A minute movement. Recent memories played in a random loop in her mind. She was running. She fell. A voice echoed in her head. Pain flashed through her entire body. She heard the voice again. She fell. More pain. She screamed . . .

On and on it went.

But the girl in the water remained motionless. She wasn't aware that her dreams were flashbacks on repeat; she experienced each one for the first time, every time. She wasn't aware that she was imprisoned. That the cable holding her captive traced its way to the middle of a gargantuan body of water in an underground cave. That right there in the centre, an elaborate structure of cables which led to more identical unmarked cocoons loomed like a derelict grand chandelier turned on its head, attached to the cave bed instead of the ceiling.

A guttural hum began, reverberating from the sinister structure as if a hidden beast in its depths was awakening from a deep slumber. Air whooshed around the cavern. The temperature plunged, causing spidery veins of frost to creep across the water's vibrating surface. The wind picked up, faster and faster—until the cable holding the girl broke the lake's surface with a splash.

The dark dripping mass hurtled towards a man. He seemed to be standing on the water, motionless but anxious. A small bluish wall lamp behind him, the only source of light in the underground chamber, outlined him with an eerie glow. His monotone outfit—dark T-shirt, backpack, jeans and sneakers—was barely visible in the dim shadow. It couldn't have been more normal, but instead of counterbalancing the otherworldliness of the cave, it served only to accent it.

Ripples from the disturbance faded some distance from the man, as if he had an invisible sphere of protection. Even the cocoon slowed when it neared him, unfurling in a deliberate manner like the unveiling of a treasure. It revealed a hint of the girl's body, pale and fragile-looking. But when the man stepped forward to receive her, the cable changed its mind and spat her out right at his feet before recoiling with haste back into the water.

Having fulfilled their task of announcing the girl's arrival, the growling and the wind died down as suddenly as they had begun.

A sheet of cold, salty air clung to the girl, teasing rebellious strands loose from hair now plastered to her face, encouraging the goosebumps to remain on her bare skin. She coughed up copious amounts of a slimy liquid that left behind a foul and sour taste in her mouth. She fought to regain control of her body as her dreams and looping memories fled with the retraction of the cable. She sputtered and shivered. Pain coursed through her huddled form like an electric current, and it joined forces with the ringing in her head. She was numb, yet in complete agony at the same time.

The seconds flew by unnoticed until a semblance of warmth returned and the girl realized she was blanketed in a soft towel. Strong hands gripped her arms and helped her to her unsteady feet.

'Keix, are you all right?'

The hushed, concerned voice sounded hesitant.

Keix . . . the word swam around in the girl's head, adding to her dizziness. It sounded strange, like the voice, yet had an out-of-reach familiarity that made her throbbing head itch. It was hard to draw connections or recall anything at all through the pain. She blinked to clear her vision. All she could make out was a rugged jawline, taut with tension. The man's face was a blur, even though she was so close to him that she could feel his breath grazing her forehead.

She tried to move away, but her legs were like deadweight. Her tongue felt like it was caked with dried mud. Fighting to control her weary limbs while trying to gather her thoughts proved too much for her emaciated body, and she would have collapsed to the floor if not for the man's support.

'Hey, stay with me!' he said. He cursed, his tone urgent but not aggressive. It sounded distant to the girl, who was trying in vain to see past the sea of stars dancing before her eyes.

The man said something else in a raised voice. The girl wasn't sure if he was talking to her because she couldn't make out the faraway words. The stars started fading, one by one, engulfed by a thick fog that was starting to envelop her other senses too. Through it, she thought she heard a rustling sound. Then she felt something like a pinprick on her arm.

Seconds later, the cold hit her like a crashing wave. Her eyes flew open and her teeth began chattering as she took in her dank and dark surroundings. An itching pain covered every part of her body. Something wasn't right—but she couldn't explain the sense of displacement she was feeling.

The numbness was leaving her body although she still couldn't stand on her own. She leaned away from the man, who was holding her steady with one hand and pushing her hair out of her face with the other, to take a proper look at him. Some of his dark hair had fallen across his forehead, framing slightly wide-set, downturned eyes, bright with worry. A single word fought an uphill battle to emerge from her. It couldn't be . . .

'Zej?' Keix's voice came out raspy, a bare whisper.

'Oh, great! I thought you would take longer to remember,' Zej said, and his shoulders relaxed a fraction.

The girl swallowed a few times, trying to moisten her throat. She didn't even remember her own name—though she had gathered enough of her wits to assume it was Keix— yet the identity of this man, this Zej, had come to her in a flash. But who was he, and what was her relationship with him? Her mind drew a blank.

'Okay . . .' Zej said hesitantly at Keix's confused look. 'I jumped the gun, didn't I? Back to the top. Yes, I am Zej. You are Keix. We've been friends for ages. You'll remember. Soon. But first, we have to get out of here.' He continued to hold on to her, but turned away and murmured something about trying.

'Keix. Friends. Out.' Keix tested the words which came out like croaks, hoping for a trace of connection to come to her like Zej's name had.

'Her brain's fried—of course, I'm sure—what do you mean I'm being hysterical?' Zej said, with his head turned slightly to the side.

Keix's mind began to fill with blurred memories. She stared at Zej's profile, analysing the slight bump on his nose bridge, the lines etched at the corner of his eye, the hardened glint of steel in dark-coloured iris and the lips pressed together in exasperation and agitation. Fragmented images of these features drawn together in anger and concern, and relaxed in a laugh flashed through her mind. Her brain strained to bring the memories into better focus.

In a sudden burst, some images sharpened and clicked into place like an unfinished puzzle. Yes, Zej was definitely a long-time friend. He was also one year her senior at Atros, the military organization they worked for. But, along with her recollections, came a stab of annoyance. Why couldn't she remember how she got here?

She pushed away from Zej and found herself staggering backwards, one foot dipping into the icy water. Her heart swooped. With impeccable accuracy, Zej threw out his hand and grabbed her flailing arm, pulling her back to the safety of the ground.

He let go of her before she could shake him off and announced through gritted teeth, 'I'm trying! You know how stubborn she can be!'

Keix's blood thrummed from her near fall and the involuntarily rising anger as she realized Zej was on an intercom with someone who knew her too. Immediately suspicious, she tried to raise her voice, but it came out hoarse and weak. 'Who are you talking to? And what is this place? Why am *I* here?'

At Keix's questioning, Zej's shoulders become stiff and straight again. 'Yep, all right. I think she's back,' Zej said to the intercom. Then he turned to face her with a tight expression.

'We should get out first,' he said, checking his watch.

Keix gave him a hard look. He held her stare for a second, then sighed.

'Okay, we're in PEER. Thousands of feet beneath it, to be exact,' he said.

Keix racked through her partially restored memories to try to place the name. Her brows snapped together. Great, her brain was coming up to speed. 'PEER?' Keix asked. 'As in . . . the Para—'

'Paranormal Electromagnetic Energy Research Centre, yes,' Zej interrupted.

A deserted underground cave that looked like it had been plucked out of an alien landscape, under one of Atros's most prestigious research facilities? How was that possible?

Zej frowned. 'The short version is, you've been imprisoned here for two years. I'm here to get you out. You have to trust me on this.'

Two years? No . . . Keix thought, *I was just . . .* what had she been doing before she had ended up here? She closed her eyes and bade the answer to come to her. But the memory seemed determined to bury itself deeper the more desperately she searched for it.

Keix swore, frustrated to nearly the point of tears. She didn't want to accept Zej's statement, but she couldn't come up with any other explanation for her situation. Her body was scraggy and clumsy—a far cry from the soldier she was supposed to be. Under the towel Zej had flung over her, her protruding ribs jabbed at arms wrapped around a concave tummy. Where once she could have fought and taken down a dozen Zejs without any sign of fatigue, she was struggling to remain upright without support, trying to will strength into her leaden limbs and not succeeding in the least.

'Look, Keix,' said Zej, startling her. 'I know you're confused. You will recover your missing memories in due course. But we have to get out of this place first. Please. Trust me.' He frowned and sighed again, taking her right arm and extending it. 'Look carefully.'

Keix stared at her arm. For a few moments, nothing happened. Just as she was about to jerk her arm back, she saw a dim pulsing orange light run the length of her arm under her skin, highlighting the green of her veins. Whatever little blood that had returned to her face, drained from it.

'Circulating trackers that are inserted in—' began Zej.

'—high-risk and condemned prisoners by Atros,' whispered Keix. Why was one of these implanted in *her* arm? Indignation filled her. The only way to get any answers was to get out of here first. She needed to find out the truth on her own. She weighed her options. It didn't look like she had any choice other than to take Zej's word at face value. Right now, he was her best bet at getting out of this dark hole.

Decision made, she watched as Zej retrieved a switchblade from his jeans.

'We have to cut it out. If we attempt to kill the signal, I'm sure Atros will be alerted,' he said apologetically. His brows snapped together in concentration as he poised the tip of the knife near Keix's wrist. When the blinking light swam back up her arm, Zej pressed down hard on the vein with his thumb to slow down the blood and keep the tracker in place. In one swift movement, he jabbed the blade into Keix's arm and flicked out the pill-shaped tracker.

Keix let out a hiss at the sudden, sharp pain. Before she knew it, Zej had pocketed the blade, produced a small cylinder, filled it with her blood and dropped the glowing tracker into it. Then he slapped a translucent piece of rubbery plaster over her wound. The cut wasn't too deep, but the plaster still turned a deep red as it soaked up her blood.

'Done,' said Zej. He tilted his head to the side and paused. 'Well, that's because she's so pale she looks like death,' he uttered with a hint of anger to the person at the other end of the intercom. Popping the cylinder into a larger silver container, he turned back to Keix. 'Anyway, this will, hopefully, keep it at body temperature so it doesn't send an alert to the control room,' he said, tossing it into the water.

'Hopefully?' Keix felt nauseous.

Zej tugged at a corner of Keix's towel and wiped off the remaining blood. The removal of the tracker seemed to have somehow reassured him. With the reflection of the low light dancing in his amused eyes, he said, 'Kidding. It'll work.' He pointed to the plaster. 'Leave that on. It'll peel off on its own when your cut has healed.'

Nodding, Keix looked around. She had partially accepted Zej's explanation that she was held prisoner by some organization, but she was going to have trouble believing that it was Atros until she could see some definitive evidence. *Besides the tracker*, she told herself. She wondered what their next step would be. There was no visible way out of the cave. Judging from the fact that Zej was dry as a bone while she was huddling under a towel for warmth, she figured that the exit probably wasn't underwater.

A rustling sound drew her attention back to Zej, who was pulling out some clothes from his backpack. 'Here, put these on,' he said, draping a pair of dark jeans and plain white T-shirt over her neck. Then he retrieved two large white coats from his bag and tossed one over his shoulder to her, before he turned around and threw his coat on. 'Wish I could have gotten you an invisibility suit, though.'

Keix suppressed a smile at the inside joke while she struggled to put on the clothes. The hooded jumpsuit which would render the wearer invisible with a single press of a button was one of Atros's breakthrough pieces of technology. She used to 'borrow' it from the restricted inventory at the Atros Training Institute, or ATI, where she had met Zej, and use it to terrorize other trainees by flipping or tripping them in the corridors. It had been her secret pastime and she had had good fun until one of them had engaged her in a spar, and, without any aid at all, had managed to win. Needless to say, she had become fast friends with this trainee—who happened to be a close friend of Zej.

'Yeah. Yeah, we're getting out now,' Zej's voice broke her out of her short reverie. 'Here are your shoes,' he turned to address her.

'Who's on the other end?' asked Keix, putting on the sneakers and appreciating the fact that her toes and feet were regaining some warmth.

'You'll find out soon enough,' replied Zej as he pulled out a triangular hoverboard from his backpack and stuffed Keix's discarded towel in before hastily pulling her towards a heavy-looking door cut into the wall of the cave. It swung open with a low buzz as they stepped through the doorway.

Keix turned back to watch the low blue light take its last dance with the fading ripples in the water cave. The next thing she knew, both of them were standing at the bottom of a long, pristinely white, cylindrical tunnel that stretched vertically above their heads with no end in sight. The door closed silently, and the wall of the tunnel smoothed over without leaving even an outline. In record time, Zej had strapped his feet to the hoverboard and was hovering in front of her. Without warning, he wrapped his arms around her and plucked her off the ground and onto the rising board.

'I wasn't going to leave you behind,' said Zej.

Keix looked up to see him cracking a crooked smile. Well, he sure had regained the cheekiness he had kept concealed from everyone except those closest to him. This moment of levity made Keix recall the time she had overheard a group of second-year girls, who hadn't known Zej, swooning over his 'coolness'. She scoffed at the memory, causing the hoverboard to bob erratically.

Zej raised a questioning eyebrow at her and she rolled her eyes in reply. She didn't want to make any sudden movements, like punching Zej, and fall off or break their only mode of transport up this seemingly never-ending vertical tunnel. The ascent would be a long one. There was no ceiling in sight and the floor was disappearing too.

Thoughts ran fast and furiously through Keix's mind. There were too many unknowns. Regardless of whether it was an Atros or enemy facility she was in, it would be foolish to draw attention to herself once she got out of this tunnel. The fact was that a tracker had been implanted into her arm, and she was convinced that the tension in Zej's shoulders wasn't fake. At this proximity, it was making her nervous too.

Once she got out of here, she needed someone other than Zej to answer her questions. She ran through the list of possible candidates in her mind and was prioritizing them when the hoverboard reached the top of the tunnel and hovered unsteadily there.

'We're waiting for our window,' Zej explained in a low whisper to Keix, then he looked to his side and frowned in concentration. 'All right. Let me know when the zone is clear.' When he turned to Keix again, he spoke in a grave tone. 'We're in one of the deepest sections of PEER. It's a maze. And the last thing we want is to draw attention to ourselves. To you. So, you'll need to do what I ask of you, all right? I'll explain everything after we get out of here.'

Keix hesitated before she gave a small nod. Her brain was still fuzzy, and her arms and legs felt like poles of lead attached to her dead trunk of a body. Even if she tried to make a run for it, she wasn't sure how far she'd get.

The hoverboard bobbed again as Zej shoved his hand into his back pocket. He retrieved a dainty necklace with a semi-polished stone charm. Keix's right hand reflexively reached up to her chest. That was where the pendant of the necklace her mother gave her always sat. The only piece of jewellery she ever wore.

Zej pressed it into her hands.

'How . . .?' Keix managed, before she stopped. Taking a steadying breath, she put the necklace into the pocket of her jeans and met Zej's eyes.

'We can do this, Keix. You can do this, *Kulcan*,' he said, using a nickname that he had given her ages ago when he had found out about her lineage.

Keix's father was a Kulcan, a fierce race of warriors, feared throughout the universe for their combat abilities.

The mention of him made her wonder where her father was right now. Few lived within the low-lying Atros city and sector boundaries. She supposed that, like the rest of his race, he preferred to stick to tradition and live up on the great heights and amid the biting-cold temperatures of mountainous areas.

Only a few people around Keix knew of her ancestry. Zej used to tease her with the name. But he had stopped when she asked him to desist. Now, the gentle reminder grounded her anxiety a little.

'Yeah, okay. Thirty-five seconds. Count it down for me,' uttered Zej. He held out a tiny skin-coloured knob in front of her. 'Pod will direct you out of here.'

Keix tried to school the surprise on her face. *Great*, she thought, *Pod, of all people*. The same trainee who had won the fight with her when she had been wearing an invisibility suit, Zej's fast friend, and the first person on the list of people she wanted to approach when she got out of this place. Her first backup plan was officially a no-go. She might have thrown up her hands in resignation if she could.

But in truth, she knew that she shouldn't have been that shocked. Pod was Zej's best friend—they were the same age, which meant that they had graduated the same year from ATI—despite the contrast in their characters. During their ATI days, Pod had even had the cheek to dub himself and Zej the Dashing (or Devastating, depending on the situation) Duo within earshot of everyone. Zej had usually settled for looking expressionless and ignoring Pod. Come to think of it, Zej would have appeared infinitely cooler just standing next to the restless and chatty Pod.

Preparing herself for a barrage of nonsense, Keix sighed and shoved the knob into her ear at Zej's urgent look.

Pod's warm voice came crisply out of the earpiece. '—teen. Twelve. You missed me, eh, *Kulcan*? Nine. Eight . . .'

Keix couldn't help but look towards the ceiling. Another thing she really shouldn't be surprised about was Pod's incessant jokes. He never got tired of them; he didn't care if others did. Mocking the nickname Zej had given Keix had been one of his favourite pastimes.

'Piss. Off,' Keix said as Pod counted down. As the ceiling opened up, she took another deep breath to steady her nerves, trying her best to will some of that legendary Kulcan strength into her deadened limbs.

2

Manipulators and Mercenaries

Keix was fuming when she made what felt like her hundred and twenty-first right turn along the winding corridors. Nothing made sense. Perhaps it was because she didn't want to believe what she was seeing, hearing or feeling. Yet somehow, everything had started to make sense with Pod's incessant commentary.

Zej's 'it's a maze' was the understatement of the year. There were no windows or glass panels in this section of PEER. Everything was white from ceiling to floor. Coupled with the fluorescent white light, it was blinding. Doors disappeared into walls as soon as they were closed. It was difficult to see where one corridor ended or rounded off. A couple of times, people wearing white coats similar to Keix's had seemingly popped out of nowhere startling her. But they barely broke pace as they strode past her. Pod, who claimed to have studied every nanometre of the blueprints continued to ramble on about how much more impressed he'd have been if he had been brought here during his field trip.

Keix had had to separate from Zej to avoid drawing attention to themselves. Because, Pod had explained, 'No one—*no one*, I repeat—in this part of PEER walks in pairs or groups'. Being alone meant that Pod was free to carry on his one-sided conversation and make observations like 'Did that guy just look at you suspiciously? You have to walk with a normal gait. Right now, you're favouring your left, and you're making this face . . . oh, is it because it's painful? I know you're rolling your eyes. Stop it or someone's going to notice. But well, you've got to keep looking on the bright side, right? I mean, you got your memory back in, like, a minute when it could have taken weeks or months. I'm just saying the Kulcan blood mojo is real, for all we know. You'll be running out of here in no time.'

Keix's fists were itching to land on something, preferably Pod's face. But all she could do was to stay silent and soldier on. It wasn't like she had any other choice because the moment she had stepped out into the empty corridor from the tunnel, a melodious voice had sounded over the earpiece, instructing her to follow Pod's instructions. Keix felt a tingling sensation that seemed to originate from under her scalp at the stranger's words. She was sure that the voice belonged to an Ifarl, a mysterious race that only interacted with its own kind. From where they lived to where they came from, everything about them was shrouded in myths.

Some rumours said that Ifarls held technologies so advanced that others could only dream of. Others told of how they were, in actual fact, huge winged creatures that could change their appearances at will. The only thing that everyone could agree on was their mind-control abilities: an Ifarl could command someone to laugh himself silly while he slaughtered his family and friends, and he would do it to a T. Or until someone managed to stop him.

Keix tried to take a left turn when Pod told her to go right at a fork. Her feet refused to do what she had tried to will herself and she glowered at her limbs' betrayal.

Pod, meanwhile, was explaining himself and giving her directions without missing a beat. 'I know you think it's excessive. But we need your absolute cooperation to get you out. Next left. And I *know* you, Keix.'

Keix had to admit that Pod was right; the temptation to do something—like sneak through a closing door—to see if she was really in PEER, was great. From the first time she had met Pod, she had sensed this inexplicable bond between them. He had just casually asked her opinion on the 'invisible menace' in the institute after their introductions, and she had given him the same story that everyone else was narrating—that she had been walking along one of the lower level corridors when an invisible force had grabbed her, flipped her on the floor and immediately vanished. But from the gleam in Pod's eyes, she had been able to tell that he knew it was her. He had affirmed her suspicions later on, seeking her out and predicting her moves almost perfectly. It was hard to impress Keix, but Pod had managed to do just that, and he had become the brother she never had.

'You have no idea how many people I approached after you went missing. No one could tell me a damn thing about where you were, what happened to you. Next right. Everyone just repeated the *official* story to me. That the soldiers stationed in Sector L had been ambushed by a highly organized rebel group. No names. No paranormal activity involved. And everyone was either dead or missing. It just didn't make sense. Okay, you have one guy coming up to your right. Walk normally, and don't make eye contact with him or talk to him.'

Pod's continued distrust should have added to Keix's anger, yet his other words were raising distant warning bells in her head. Why had she been in Sector L? Who had died? Keix's heart pounded more forcefully at that thought. Zej said she had been here for two years. What exactly had happened in that time? Her headache returned with fresh intensity, refusing to let her mind answer her questions. She couldn't even place her most recent memory.

As far as Keix knew, Atros city and its clearly divided sectors provided a safe environment for people to live in; the crime rate was nearly zero and everyone existed in harmony. In return for its citizens' obedience, Atros trained and deployed soldiers to keep any threats to their safety at bay. It was a system that worked. Which was why rebel groups were few and far between. Keix hadn't ever heard of an organized one, much less one that could ambush Atros's soldiers successfully. Was the news of their increasing power and influence hiding in one of her missing memories? If she could trust Pod, her next question was: Why would Atros put out a false story?

Why would they put a tracker in you and keep you imprisoned underwater? a small voice in Keix's mind asked.

She tried to calm her breathing and to relax her shoulders as she watched, out of the corner of her eye, a bald bespectacled man with beady eyes and a greasy nose amble past. She barely suppressed a gasp when she saw an Atros logo pinned to the upper left side of his white coat. At that very moment, their eyes met and Greasy Nose's eyes widened a fraction. Keix tensed. She clenched her fists, but he threw a small nod in her direction and continued walking, muttering to himself.

Oblivious to Keix's racing heart, Pod continued talking. 'So I approached Zej . . .' he paused for a moment, before continuing awkwardly, 'er . . . anyway, I was running into dead ends, even with my genius hacking and surveillance skills. Next right, through the first door on your left—I'm opening it for you now so you can see it—and down two flights of stairs. Then Zej . . . he sort of found out where you were. I'll leave it to him to tell you how. I didn't believe it in the beginning. I mean . . . Atros holding you prisoner then putting out a phoney story to the public? That, and some other things—nothing added up. So I had to find out if it was true. Never miss a chance to dig deeper, right?'

Well, that's probably the first thing we've agreed on since I got out of the tunnel, thought Keix.

'And next thing I knew, I had these blueprints showing underground levels and building extensions in PEER that the official ones don't. And I was looking at the corridors, seeing people entering and exiting doors in these sections that supposedly don't exist through real-time camera feeds. It was beyond insane! The rooms themselves—and the underground prison you just came out from—don't have camera surveillance. What do you think they are doing inside, though? Anyway, the corridors have cameras, of course. If they didn't, I don't think we would have gotten this far. Next right.'

Keix took the next right. This corridor was no different from the one she had just left. Everything was white—the pristine floor, the walls that sloped inwards at the top and the ceiling interspersed with square vents—and sterile.

'I mean, if this much was hidden from us, what makes you think that the stories about chimera behemoths aren't—Wait, damn! Stay where you are! I've got three guards heading in your direction. They're doing a sweep!' Static noises came through the intercom, interrupting Pod's panicked voice. 'Why . . . doing . . . time . . . it's not—'

Then there was dead silence. Blood drummed in Keix's ears as she saw three figures moving towards her. Ranged shoulder to shoulder, they took up the entire width of the corridor. Revulsion overcame her when she realized that they were Odats, the foulest kind of mercenaries with limited intelligence and inexhaustible physical strength.

Their skin was a dark mustard yellow, and their squat faces looked identical. Narrow eyes underlined thick straight brows, and above a wide thin-lipped mouth sat a broad nose with flared nostrils. With her heightened senses, courtesy of her Kulcan blood, Keix could smell an undertone of fetidness that was masked with a thick layer of disinfectant. Someone must have bothered enough—and succeeded in the attempt—to get these creatures cleaned up for duty.

The Odats' guard uniforms, emblazoned with the Atros logo, were made to blend into their surroundings. But their broad and muscular bodies weren't, resulting in a bizarre and unnerving intermittent wave-like effect when they moved. It was as if part of the wall at the end of the corridor had warped and was closing in on her. Keix was surprised to hear only the thudding of their boots and an occasional squeak against the spotless floor despite their size.

Keix had never encountered an Odat in person, but her training at ATI had covered these repulsive creatures extensively enough. She recalled a class in which the trainees were shown a video to let them know exactly what the Odats were—and were not—capable of. One of them had cornered a civilian, and someone off-camera was screaming at it to tie the person up. The directive was lost on the brute, which approached its victim and started tearing him limb from limb. With every scream the man let out, the Odat would shudder in pleasure. But that wasn't all. The beast went on to shove the man's remains into its toothless jaws, grinding and swirling them around before swallowing.

'You need to know what you will be up against once you graduate,' their class instructor had told the sea of horrified fifteen-year-old faces looking up at him when the video ended.

Years had passed since then, but the same look of horror found its way back to Keix's face. Why would PEER engage Odats as guards, much less have anything to do with them? Her pulse quickened and her throat dried up.

Keix looked around. Was there a security protocol—a pass she had to flash, or a codeword to mutter to show that she was *supposed* to be here? She tried to move but found herself rooted to the spot. *Crap! Did that idiot Pod tell me to stay where I am?* She let out a low growl, which alerted the burly triplets to her presence.

'You.' The word came out deep and raspy.

Keix supposed it might have come from the Odat in the middle. Its mouth had parted a little wider than the others. She pretended not to hear it to try to buy time as the eerie ripple continued to close in on her. She flexed her arms and legs, testing their agility and readying herself for a fight.

Not one word or gesture was exchanged between the ugly creatures as they concentrated on their task, but all three now had their eyes focused on her. As the triplets drew near, someone came up from behind her. She turned just in time to see Zej running to them with an outstretched arm, his chest heaving.

'You three! You're needed on Level H, Area I,' he shouted, gesturing to the area behind the Odats.

The figures paused in unison. Keix held her breath. She couldn't tell from their stony expressions whether they understood what Zej said. He seemed to have the same thought as he repeated his instructions, enunciating each word.

The guard in the middle moved towards Zej. It rasped, 'We do not take orders from you.' Keix was so astonished at its articulation she almost fell over.

There was a split second of tension when everyone seemed to be frozen in time. Then, the Odat who spoke extended its fist towards Zej's head. Keix saw the movement and reached out to intercept it instinctively. She grabbed its outstretched wrist and punched its temple, making it stumble backwards. Zej landed a kick on its chest. The combined force sent the Odat flying backwards with a grunt.

The shock on its comrades' faces quickly changed to menacing expressions.

'I'll take the one on the right,' Keix called out to Zej, throwing all caution to the wind now that the shit had hit the fan. The chances of them getting out without a fight were zero to none.

Keix turned her attention to the Odat on her right. She struck a kick at its waist, followed by a punch to its nose. The brute turned out to be steadier on its feet than its fallen friend, but its fighting tactics left much to be desired. Instead of a coordinated attack, it swung its arms out in a random manner, hoping to make contact with her. Breathing heavily, it uttered a low cry with each move.

Keix dodged the clumsy manoeuvres with more effort than she would have normally used, as her body took longer to respond to her commands. The Odat's lousy strategy paid off when its elbow connected with her shoulder. Atros might be lying about certain things, but the note on an Odat's strength was not one of them. With this single touch, piercing pain shot up her shoulder. The impact flung her against the wall where she hit her other shoulder and head and crumpled to the floor.

The first guard that they had taken out was now back on its feet. It turned its attention to Zej. Out of the corner of her eye, Keix saw Zej backing away from the two guards.

His agility was giving him the upper hand. The guards were clumsy and always two seconds too slow to get their hands on him.

Keix struggled to stand, but she had lost all control over her limbs. Just as she saw the Odat's face closing in on her, she felt a small spark at the back of her skull. As quickly as it formed, it spread out into tiny threads which fizzled out. But the inexplicable sensation seemed to have restored her strength. She kicked out at her opponent's shins and scrambled to the side.

A boot stamped down beside her hip and a crack appeared on the floor. The Odat she was fighting was looking to crush her alive now. It raised its leg again. A high-pitched ringing pierced the air right then. At the distraction, it wobbled comically for a moment. Three successive hisses sounded, and the guard fell backwards. Keix looked up to see Zej holding a gun, still directed at the spot where her opponent had been standing just seconds ago. At his feet were the other two Odats, unconscious.

Before Keix could say a word, Zej said, 'Don't look so shocked. Two years of specialized training—you would have done better than me, if you had that.'

Zej helped Keix up and the two of them looked around. The commotion couldn't have gone unnoticed. And since someone—possibly the two of them—had set off the blaring alarm, the place would be swarming with guards soon.

Keix stood up and looked to Zej for directions since Pod was still offline. 'Where to next? I lost Pod when there was static interference just now.'

'Me too. They must have jammed the outside signals,' Zej said, looking around in frustration. 'I can't lead you out of here without Pod's help. Especially now that the alarm is triggered.'

As soon as Zej finished his sentence, the siren stopped and a robotic female voice announced: 'All staff, please gather at your respective emergency meeting points. An alarm has been triggered on Level H, Area I. Guard units within a two-area radius, please respond. All other units, remain on standby.'

Zej appeared relieved at the announcement. 'Pod must have set off the alarm as distraction. We agreed on the Level and Area in case something went wrong. This couldn't have been a coincidence.'

But before either of them could discuss their next move, they heard footsteps hurrying in their direction.

'Quick, you need to hide. Not in plain sight this time,' Zej said. He looked up, gesturing to a small grille above them. 'Hurry, the vent.' He clasped his fingers together to create a step for Keix. With the additional boost, it was easy for her to reach up and push the vent cover aside. But her shoulder screamed in protest when she tried to pull herself into the small space. Sensing her difficulty, Zej gave her another push. Her feet had barely cleared the opening when a person appeared around the corner.

Keix peeked through the opening and saw that it was Greasy Nose. He paused for a moment, taking in the scene before him. Confusion evident in his face, he asked Zej, 'I thought the alarm was set off on Level H, Area I?'

To Zej's credit, he looked as bewildered as Greasy Nose as he answered, 'I'm not sure too. I came this way and saw these three on the ground. I think I saw a shadow disappear around that corner.' He gestured to the other end of the corridor.

Greasy Nose's breathing quickened at the news. His thin voice trembled a little when he said, 'The intruder was here? We should head for the meeting point and inform the rest!'

Seeing that there was no way out of this without raising further suspicion, Zej nodded and followed him along.

Watching their retreating backs, Keix replaced the grille with as little noise as she could. The vent was white too, like the corridors under it. The only difference was that, instead of claustrophobic walls, it had an extremely low ceiling that required her to remain in a crouch. She stayed deathly still, numbness creeping into her limbs. It felt like ages had passed in silence after the alarm was switched off, and the corridor continued to remain empty. There was still only radio silence from Pod.

Suddenly, a woman's wail echoed through the vent tunnel.

What else was Atros hiding? Curiosity battled caution, but a gnawing feeling urged her to investigate. Gingerly, she moved, bit by bit, towards the sound. It felt as though Pod's last command that she stay put was no longer valid. But it didn't seem wise to make a bid for freedom right now, considering the fact that she had no idea *how* exactly to get out of here.

By the time she had crawled through the vent to reach the origin of the cry and glanced down the slits in the vent cover, she was seriously re-evaluating her limited trust in Zej and Pod's words.

Handcuffed by her wrists to chains attached to opposite corners of the ceiling was a girl, her cheekbones made prominent by malnutrition. Her hair was matted in places and so dirty that the colour was indiscernible except for a hint of pink. One half of it was much longer than the other. But as sorry a state as the girl was in, her eyes were bright and intelligent. And they were looking straight in the direction of the vent, boring right into Keix's eyes.

No, it can't be, Keix tried to reassure herself. Another memory clicked into place. This girl looked like her best friend. But her best friend was dead. She had seen it happen. She had killed Vin.

When Keix heard Vin speaking in her head, she jumped. Her head hit the top of the vent and a clang reverberated through the narrow tunnel. Vin's usually sweet voice sounded harsh over mindspeak. 'Keix! Get out of here now. We'll meet again when the time is right. Go!' Just like before, when Pod's Ifarl associate had commanded her to follow his instructions, the tingling sensation in Keix's scalp returned. She knew that Vin was half-Ifarl, but her friend had never exhibited or spoken of any abilities that she might have inherited from her enigmatic ancestors— except before she died, Keix recalled now.

With Vin's orders firmly in place, Keix found herself scrambling down the vent in no particular direction when all she wanted to do was to jump down into the room and grill her friend on how and why she was still alive. The exertion made her breathe heavily, and her breaths created mists that swirled for a second or two before fading away in the freezing vent. When she was some distance away from Vin's room, Pod's voice came back on over the earpiece. She swallowed audibly, tasting the lingering unpleasantness in her mouth.

'You're in the vent, aren't you? How come you're further away than where we lost contact?' Pod asked.

Keix pondered about telling Pod about Vin, but some part of her wanted to keep it a secret—at least until she got some answers herself and figured out how to stop her mind from reeling from all her recent discoveries.

Misinterpreting her hesitation, Pod said, 'Ah, you don't want tell me. That's fine. Losing contact and popping up somewhere else can be considered a type of leverage, I think. Anyway, I'm not really into leverage and that sort of nonsense. I prefer getting due credit for my genius. So I'm going to confess that I sounded the alarm to distract the Odat guards so you could get into the vent. How did I know? Because the vent is Plan C. Remember what we said about your favourite *Plan C*? That it's the fastest and riskiest one.' Pod sniffed, trying to sound disapproving. 'Luckily I had help switching off the lasers before you climbed in. You really like your lasers, don't you? Got to remind us that you were the only trainee in the history of ATI to ace the laser obstacle course—even in a time like this . . .'

'The vent was Zej's idea,' Keix hissed in irritation.

'What?' Pod sounded genuinely shocked at that revelation. He swore and then his tone changed completely when Keix told him what happened with the Odats. 'You need to pick up speed. Once the guards wake up, Zej's cover will be blown. We need to get you both out of there before that happens—if it hasn't already.'

The flurry of tapping sounds at Pod's end increased in intensity while he gave Keix directions tersely. Trying to move through the vent without making any noise proved to be a huge challenge, especially when there were so many Odats patrolling the corridors underneath her.

The extreme cold in the vent was getting to her even though it kept her body from shutting down. But mostly, it was only through the sheer act of placing one hand and one foot before the other that she managed to make it all the way to rendezvous with an anxious-looking Zej in the garage.

Keix knew that being able to make it this far out of the facility without being caught—despite the earlier alert—was testament to Pod's wizardry with systems. When she eventually dropped down from the vent, thoughts randomly surfaced in her swimming head: she was sparring with Zej on the hoverboard and managed to give him a black eye; Vin was using mindspeak to scream at her, blaming her for her predicament and she couldn't answer back because she was chained up in the vent, gagged, with lasers pointing at her and alarms blaring; she was back in the underground prison, alone and drowning.

A wave of nausea washed over her and she collapsed onto the garage floor. The last thing she saw was Zej running towards her. There was no fighting the irresistible call to close her eyes and drift into nothingness.

3

Memories

Keix awoke in a dream. A memory. She knew it was one because of the unmistakable sense of déjà vu that the scene evoked. Every detail had a glaze over it, making it blurrier, yet somehow more polished than real life. She also had this odd sense of displacement, as if she were both a viewer and a participant at the same time; her brain must be compensating for the temporary loss of this last piece of her memory with clarity and heightened perception.

Facing a white wall, Keix was standing to attention in a room with concrete flooring. About thirty other Atros soldiers were with her, many of them fresh graduates, lined up in rows of five.

Oron, their overall mentor and head trooper, was projected in the empty space in front of the wall as a hologram. The three-dimensional projection was so defined and detailed that it looked like he was physically in the room with Keix and the other soldiers.

As usual, Oron looked impeccable in his combat uniform and trademark black cape that drew attention to his broad shoulders, giving him an imposing air. Two streaks of silver at his temples paired with his piercing grey eyes emphasized his crown of spiky black hair.

Keix had always thought he was incredibly stylish and amusing even though her fellow trainees had never agreed with the latter assessment; in their words, 'If amusing was spelt, M-E-N-A-C-I-N-G, then yes, Oron is as amusing as hell'.

'Atros soldiers,' Oron said in his booming voice, addressing the room. 'I know that this is the first field assignment for many of you. It is *not* an excuse to mess around. You know your positions and roles. Stick to them. Your seniors are not your minders. Don't expect them to baby you. It's time to put what you have learned to use. Do *not* sully Atros's reputation. As full-fledged Atros troopers, you are expected to conform to the highest standards.' His eyes swept across the room. 'At all times,' he added.

Keix peeked to her side. Vin, standing beside her, looked very far from being the skeleton she had just seen in PEER. Her shoulder-length hair was shocking pink and parted to one side. The other side of her head was shaved to reveal an intricate tattoo-like pattern of interweaving pink lines to show her lineage as a half-Ifarl. Both her hair and tattoo were sharp contrasts against her pale skin and the green and brown utilitarian-looking suit she was wearing.

Catching Keix's eye, Vin gave her a mischievous wink.

'Now, I know many of you think that nothing interesting—paranormal or not—ever happens in Sector

L because it is so far removed from the main city,' Oron continued, now from one end of the room to another, between the ranks. 'Some of you may have celebrated your luck at being assigned this rotation, thinking that you'll get to kick back and party for the next three months. Others may be upset because you think that you won't get to kick some ghostly ass.'

Keix smirked at Vin. She could have sworn that Oron's gaze lingered on the two of them: Life-(and host, usually)-of-the-party Vin and first-in-line-in-any-mission Keix.

A number of recruits cast shifty glances around while some tried to hide their unease behind a soft cough or clearing of throat. The seniors stared straight ahead, their expressions stoic.

'*But* I am here to disappoint all of you,' said Oron. His demeanour got more serious—something Keix never thought was possible. He waved his arm and a map of Atros's main city and its sectors appeared behind him. Spots in various colours appeared on the sector borders. 'This is as much of a welcome message as it is a briefing. Paranormal activities, as well as skirmishes conducted by our enemies, have been increasing in frequency in these past months. Sector L has remained fairly quiet, but that doesn't mean that we can lower our guard. In fact, we have to step up patrols so we won't be taken unawares. Is that clear?'

'Yes, Sir Oron,' chorused the troopers without hesitation. Everyone had stood up a little straighter at the news of recent attacks.

'Schedules have been distributed, so I trust that every one of you has memorized them by heart. You are divided into two units, conducting patrols on a rotating roster. Remember, if both units have to be dispatched in case of an emergency, Control has to be informed.' On this ominous note, Oron pressed a button on his wrist and his hologram, together with the map, flashed and converged into a small bright spot in the middle of the wall before disappearing.

Silence reigned for a second following the abrupt dismissal before everyone realized that the briefing was over and broke ranks.

Keix flung her arm around Vin and asked in a hushed voice, 'What do you think of that, huh?'

Vin tilted her head. 'Well, considering that Atros disseminates its information on a need-to-know basis, I would say it's pretty serious,' she frowned.

Keix nodded. A trace of unease crept through her. She tried to school her thoughts even though part of her felt a rush of excitement at the thought of getting to taste some action. Still, she didn't want to let on that Oron's words had bothered her more than she would admit.

Sensing her mood, Vin interrupted her. 'Well, there's nothing we can do about it, except have a little fun before my next shift, right?'

Keix laughed. Vin's motto in life was always party first, worry later.

Smiling, they filed out with the rest of the recruits into a large sitting area.

Just like the briefing room, it had a concrete floor and whitewashed walls. A lemony scent filled the room. Stark fluorescent lights bordered the ceiling and divided it into half. Splashes of colour in the form of mismatched throw pillows littered the massive white sofas. A knitted banner with the words 'Welcome to the Twin Lounges' hanging above a long and large screen added some liveliness to the otherwise antiseptic space. A slow, jazzy tune flitted through the room.

Most of the troopers seemed to be of the same mind as Vin. Chatter soon drowned the background music as the more rambunctious seniors tried to convince the newbies that they could get drunk on a drink that looked and tasted suspiciously like fruit punch. Some left for their quarters to rest, but Keix stayed on with the others, reminiscing about their exploits at ATI and speculating on what dangers they would encounter in the other sectors.

The space became considerably less crowded and messier after Vin's group left for their scheduled patrol. Out of boredom, Keix had taken to crushing the empty cans strewn around and tossing them into the trash bin in a corner of the room.

Keix was on her last can when a low urgent beeping sounded. A detached voice boomed: 'Paranormal activity detected two-point-six miles from the West Wing, Exit R. Activity level: high.'

Everyone jumped to attention. Even those who had been passed out on the sofas until a few seconds ago sprang into action. Soldiers marched from their rooms as their training took precedence over any amount of panic and inebriation that they might have felt.

Lyndon, a tall and brawny senior who had been assigned to lead the group that Keix was in, stepped into the centre of the room. His clothes were crumpled, having been slept in, but his eyes were alert and refreshed. 'Unit B, you have thirty seconds to change into your uniforms and grab your weapons. We'll meet at the entrance hall and proceed to check out the area.'

The announcement sounded again. Lyndon turned to Keix and said, 'Keix, you are to inform Control. We'll be heading out from Exit R. Catch up after you're done.'

Keix bit down a protest. Troopers were trained to follow orders first.

As the rest of the soldiers moved out of the sitting room, Lyndon whispered to her. 'Just so you know, I assigned you the hardest role. Also, I know you'll be able to catch up faster than any of the rest.'

Keix was a little taken aback but mollified by his words. Lyndon, with his strict bearing and no-nonsense attitude, used to cast her and Vin exasperated looks whenever they got caught in some kind of mischief during their ATI days. It was no secret that the two girls called him an Oron wannabe both behind his back and to his face. Despite that, he always treated them with cool and polite bemusement. Giving him a knowing nod, Keix made a mental note to herself to revisit her original assessment of him.

Not wanting to waste time, Keix ran back into her room and changed into her combat gear before entering one of the broad corridors that led to the control room. She walked past a series of identical doors to the end and placed her palm on a spot on the wall. The delayed activation of the mechanism served to thwart unauthorized visitors and others who did not know troopers' protocol, a necessary precaution that seemed nothing but counterproductive to Keix right now.

Thirty seconds later, there was a gentle hiss and the entire wall moved backwards, opening a gap just wide enough for Keix to scoot into the room sideways. The control room, which ran on autopilot most of the time, was empty as expected. It was as large as the sitting room and its walls, except the doorway, were covered in grid-like images from ceiling to floor. Some of them were surveillance feeds, but there were others that displayed sonar images and three-dimensional spike graphs. The images on the screens showing the area west of the sector post were fading in and out erratically—an almost-sure sign of paranormal disturbance.

Keix turned her attention to the table in the middle of the room where a virtual mass of odd shapes was floating above it. She stepped up to it and started moving the shapes around with her hands, rearranging them precisely even though there was no tactile feedback. When the puzzle was solved, the pieces disappeared and the words 'Sector L' flashed bright. Keix tapped a few buttons to connect to Control but the connection kept suggesting that there was no one at the receiving end. Assuming that the signal was jammed due to the disturbance, she gathered all the data from before the alert sounded and packaged it into a high-priority message for Control. The system would send it out as soon as the signalling problem resolved itself.

Once Keix was done, she sprinted out of the building. Before long, she was racing down a narrow dirt road in a lightly forested area. The lavender flush of the approaching dusk had taken on a pinkish tinge. Through the heavy woody scent that permeated the air, she could sense an odd tension, like the frenzied buzzing of an insect aware of its nearing end.

Distant shouts informed Keix that she was approaching the fray and she worked her legs harder. Nothing in ATI prepared her for the sight that met her eyes—it was one that outstripped even the most outrageous prediction from the most creative or boastful trooper about what they could possibly come up against. And it sent chills right down to her bones.

In the middle of the track was a translucent sphere formed by dozens of intermingling bluish human-like apparitions. Glowing red orbs speckled with amber and green bordered it. The huge shape looked like a growing, quivering soap bubble. Through it, Keix could see her teammates—dark shadows moving in and out of focus in the shifting ball.

Bodies were strewn outside of the bubble, their eyes wide open and unfocused, faces frozen in horror and misery as if they were trapped in a trance. The sight might have been bewitching if it hadn't been so eerie.

Keix was reminded of what Oron had said in one of her first lectures. 'Ghosts bring forth pain when they touch your bare skin. With that connection, their worst memories become yours—that much we know from people who have experienced this. This transference of energy strengthens the spirits. Orbs glow brighter, eventually gaining some semblance of human form; spirits which already have a form become less translucent. Some witnesses' accounts say the ghosts "grinned and looked high". So it's speculated that ghosts are in a constant state of pain and this "feeding" gives them relief from that agony,' he explained with thinned lips to a class of newbies, his disapproval of the conjectures clear. 'While we cannot replicate the passing on of memories, all of you will be subjected to a pain tolerance test before you are deemed fit to graduate. That will be your first taste of what it feels like to be attacked. And even if you pass the test'—his lips became almost non-existent—'it means nothing in a real combat situation.'

Keix paled at the memory of the excruciating agony that had struck her to her very core when she had gone through the test. She stiffened and wrenched her thoughts back to the scene in front of her.

She hesitated as she looked for a weak spot to attack. For a moment, the shape seemed to disperse and Keix caught sight of Vin, Lyndon and what was left of their two units. They kept their backs to one another in formation and were shooting cast nets from their guns. Keix saw someone fire yet another one. It flew out from the muzzle with a hiss, white, luminous and needle-sharp, before expanding out wide in all directions. True to its purpose, the trap covered a cluster of spectres and balled up. But like the previous ones, it exploded under the sheer stress from the number of spirits it was trying to contain, flickering before losing its glow.

Keix watched, helpless, her frustration growing. The orbs and apparitions were closing in on them ferociously. Vin and Lyndon were shouting commands, their voices becoming distorted by the time they reached Keix even though she wasn't that far away.

The only weapon that could reduce their enemies' numbers was the black hole bullet which would suck in the enemies into nothingness to ensure they would never come back again. But with so many of them weaving around her fellow soldiers, there was no guarantee that her teammates wouldn't be pulled into the portal too. They would be as good as dead if they were drawn into the hole.

Keix stalked the edge of the battle, trying to find an opening. She squinted at the glaring light coming from the huge ball, which seemed to glow brighter with every falling soldier. The unearthly creatures were determined to tear the soldiers apart.

Despite her unwillingness to sacrifice anyone, her training told her that she had to cut their losses. Atros soldiers' first and foremost duty was to protect the people living within the sectors. A group like this could easily overrun a small-sized town, gaining momentum as it swept through Sector L towards the centre of the city. She had never heard of ghosts banding together like that. Ever.

Atros needed to know about this dangerous anomaly. The information that she had sent back to Control hadn't even come close to conveying a tenth of the destruction that this ball could potentially bring.

Damn it, thought Keix viciously, why couldn't someone come up with a communication device that worked around ghosts and was unaffected by their energy?

She retrieved a small pistol from the back of her waistband and leapt forward. Taking cover behind the thick trunk of a tree, she took aim as the struggle continued.

The supernatural bubble grew steadily bigger, and the buzzing grew louder. Her hands and breathing remained steady, as if completely unaffected by her surroundings and previous physical exertion, while her pistol stayed trained on the furthest point of the ball. She narrowed her eyes and squeezed the trigger at her first window of opportunity. The bullet made contact with the last red glowing point of the phantoms.

The point pulsed for a moment before expanding rapidly into a dark ball that took up the entire spectrum of Keix's vision. Everything that had existed within the sphere a millisecond before—the blue, red, orange and green glowing apparitions and orbs, a lone tree, grass, pebbles, stones, and grit and dirt included—was drawn to its core, distorting like an ethereal perspective drawing and vanishing with an audible swoosh.

The impact of the implosion stunned the remaining ghosts, and Keix caught sight of the few troopers who were still standing, including Vin.

'Run, Keix!' Vin's voice pierced through the just-hollowed air. Her voice worked like a shrill alarm, reanimating the remaining spirits. The split second of distraction proved costly as an icy blue apparition of a human girl with hair that was as long as she was tall moved in and touched a finger softly to Vin's cheek.

The fight drained out of Vin's eyes even as they bore into Keix's. When Vin's compulsion came, Keix was shocked, having never experienced anything like it before. Even though Vin's voice was weak and fleeting, a whisper in her head, the power of the enchantment was not diminished.

'Fire. Then run.' The order crept into Keix's head as the intensity of the pain flashed in Vin's eyes before they slammed shut.

Keix fought to disobey Vin's command. More spectres were flooding in to replace those that had been dispatched through the black hole. Where were they coming from?

Her finger tightened on the trigger involuntarily as she saw the remaining soldiers, including Lyndon, drop to the ground one by one as the enemies swarmed them. The orbs leaned in close to their victims, basking in their life. Some of them gained mass, transforming into nebulous human forms. These ones clawed at the exposed skin of the troopers, clinging on as if this touch was their only lifeline, greedily feeding on the energy of the living.

Keix turned and ran after the bullet left her gun. She didn't and couldn't stay to witness her best friend disappear from the face of the universe.

The scene shifted before Keix could catch her breath. She was in another memory. With the same hazy, yet polished effect. The same extraordinary clarity to the details. The same intensity of perception.

Now, she was wedged between two Odats, her arms bound behind her back, her ankles tied together so tightly she couldn't feel her toes. The creatures were holding her up with vice-like grips on her upper arms, dragging her along a brightly lit corridor. They could have been the same ones she had fought in PEER. She couldn't tell. From their inanimate yellow-green pupils encircled by a thin black iris down to the undertone of rotting breath, it was as if these savages were impersonal clones.

'Where are you taking me?' Keix asked, panic and shock evident in her voice. 'I've already given my account! The package I sent from Sector L to Control is evidence that we were attacked by a large group of ghosts—not rebels!' She tried to throw the guards off by twisting her body, but they must have injected her with something. Her muscles felt feeble and refused to react.

Unfazed by Keix's shouting, the guards continued to tug her along the doorless hallway.

'I need to see Oron. I want to see Oron. NOW! O-RON!' Keix screamed right into one of the guards faces, which probably wasn't the best idea; the next thing she knew, she felt a prick followed by a cooling sensation at the side of her neck and her eyelids slid down of their own accord.

Keix woke up to find herself still restrained, except now she was secured upright with a rigid board biting into her back. Suspended in mid-air, spotlights blazed on her from an unseen height and she averted her eyes. Her clothes were clinging to every inch of her body and water coursed down to the tip of her bare toes and dripped into the pool beneath her.

Her hair was wet, plastered to her face. The opposite of her parched throat. Keix's hoarse voice came out a bare whisper. 'Where am I? What are you doing to me?' She addressed the empty space as her teeth chattered.

The response that came didn't directly answer her questions, but it was enough to make her heart clench. A dispassionate voice announced through the blinding light:

'Trial 24. Extend by two-point-five seconds. Total time: Two minutes and thirty-three seconds.'

A whirring followed the announcement. Before Keix could make any sense of it, she was plunged into the freezing water. She gasped. Salty, bitter water forced its way into her open mouth. Keix gurgled and swallowed the foul liquid as her throat constricted in resistance. The residual lights that were etched onto the back of her eyelids dimmed, obscured by a thickening haze. Her hands and feet spasmed against her restraints, but there was no escaping them.

Keix was warm and dry again. All she could see was white. She wasn't sure if it was from spotlights shining directly into her eyes or just the colour scheme of the room. She thought she felt blisters on her back. Was it from the constant rubbing of her skin against the board? *At least I'm lying down now so the straps are not cutting into my arms and legs.* She heard a cough. It sounded close to laughter. She was delirious. Pain and pleasure seemed to be indistinguishable.

Turn it up higher, she begged. It was too much trouble to split her cracked lips again to speak to someone who she wasn't at all confident was there. Also, she doubted whether she could voice her thoughts. Even if she could muster up enough strength to swallow, she had no saliva left to soothe the desert that was occupying the inside of her throat.

She heard the robotic voice from before again: 'Trial 107. Repeat voltage. Extend exposure time by one second.

Total time: Four minutes and three seconds. Two shocks.'
Closing her eyes to a sunny yellow-orange landscape with white dancing globes, Keix waited for something that she never thought she would wish for in her life—oblivion.

4

Revelations

When she awoke, Keix couldn't tell if it was day or night. For a split second, she thought she was back in the torture chamber. But the smell of old wood mingled with soap reassured her otherwise. She sat up and looked around. A single light bulb dangled from the ceiling. It emitted a soft, flickering orange glow that illuminated a tiny, windowless room. The bed she was in looked old but sturdy. It stood in the corner and was the only piece of furniture in the room.

Keix took deep breaths to soothe her frayed senses. She attempted to organize the sudden deluge of memories. The remnants of her dream made her reflexively rub her wrists. Thin faded lines that had never been there before encircled them. She reached to touch her naked back and felt calluses where her shoulder blades and spine jutted out.

She was trying to make sense of what had happened since her escape from PEER, her revived recollections and her weakened body when a piece of neon-coloured paper caught her attention. It was sitting atop a stack of clothes at the foot of the bed.

You stink. Take a shower. Talk when we get back. Pod.

Keix almost snorted. The signature was unnecessary. She could recognize Pod's childish handwriting anywhere.

She sniffed herself. Soured sweat and an undertone of stale vomit lurked beneath a run-of-the-mill soap fragrance. She couldn't remember getting cleaned up—on her own or with someone's help. *Maybe this is one of those things that I would be better off not knowing*, she thought.

There were two doors in the room, which she opened in succession. One led to a dim corridor with a flight of stairs at the end. The other opened into an en-suite bathroom half the size of the adjoining bedroom.

Despite the urge to escape or determine where she was, Keix decided that she'd fare better with confrontations if she gave herself a bit more time to feel more like her old self. She stepped into the shower and drank a few mouthfuls of the tepid water to ease her sore throat.

It was a miracle that she and Zej had managed to escape PEER at all. He must have carried her into his car and driven out of the compound before the guards they fought had woken up.

Keix had a sudden epiphany. What if Atros had classified her as a mole because they had found evidence that Sector L's attack was carried out by a rebel group? *But what about the ghosts? Did the attacks overlap? Or were they working together?* Keix shook her head, sending a spray of suds over the walls. The implausibility of this theory was staggering.

Still, Control must have sent backup over in time to defeat the ghosts. Otherwise, Sector L would have been overrun and city-wide panic would have ensued.

But how had Vin survived the black hole bullet? Keix was sure that her friend had been within the bullet's range when she had fired. Did Atros suspect that Vin was working for the rebels too? At the thought of her underwater prison, Atros hiring Odats and the torture they had put her through, Keix shuddered—it was a side of the organization she had never known existed. She wondered if the torture had broken her, if she had told them exactly what they wanted to hear. Also, since Pod and Zej had broken her out of Atros's custody, surely they must now be classified as rebels too?

Still fretting over whether there was any way to prove her innocence and justify her friends' actions, Keix finished her shower and put on the clothes in the pile. The white T-shirt and muslin drawstring pants were worn, but clean and comfortable. She felt thankful, although a little weirded out that either Pod or Zej had been thoughtful enough to provide brand-new undergarments as well. After she had slipped on a pair of canvas shoes—also new, from the look of them—she stepped out of the room. Approaching the foot of the stairs, she noticed a larger sitting area through an empty door frame.

She wrinkled her nose at the faintly mouldy smell of the room while feeling for a light switch on the side of the door frame. When the lights came on, she almost jumped back in shock to see Zej seated on an ancient-looking armchair. He was twiddling something between his fingers, lost in thought. The chair had patches and dark stains on its upholstery and was backed up against one of the peeling khaki wallpaper-covered walls. The rest of the spartan furniture included a grey-blue plastic low stool, a wooden chair, a metal bar stool, and a wooden rectangular coffee table that had been flipped on its shorter side to make space for the only modern-looking article in the room: a control table similar to the one Keix had operated in Sector L's secret room.

'Hey,' Zej said without missing a beat. He stood up and shoved the thing he had been fiddling with into his jeans pocket. There was a five o'clock shadow along his jaw, but his damp hair and crisp T-shirt indicated that he, too, had recently cleaned up. The zesty scent of soap that Keix's sensitive nose caught confirmed as much.

'What's with the sitting in the dark thing?' Keix asked by way of greeting.

Zej smiled and glanced at his watch. 'You're finally up. How are you feeling? Pod and the rest went to get some supplies. They should be back soon.'

Keix nodded and took a step forward and found her knees buckling at the simple movement. She gave a cry of shock, raising both hands to break her fall. Zej rushed forward to help her, only to end up banging his hip against the bar stool, knocking it over and going down with it. They both ended up face down, inches from one another.

'Not that good, I guess,' said Keix from her prostrate position. She laughed while pushing herself up. She looked over at Zej, who was doing the same. The last and only time they had ended up in this position was when Pod and

Vin had bet against each other that their respective best friends would hang on longer on the spinning log during their standard obstacle course training. Keix would have been the last one standing if Pod hadn't 'accidentally' pushed her off the bar when Zej looked like he was falling off. She didn't know if Zej was remembering this too when he gave her an amused grin and scrambled to his feet.

'You should sit down,' Zej said. He led Keix to the armchair that he had vacated. Pulling up the low stool, he sat himself a short distance away from her as she uttered her thanks.

A short silence followed as Keix wondered where to begin.

Zej broke the silence first. 'Hey, before they get back . . .' he said, standing up and pulling out the item he had previously stuck into his pocket. It was the necklace that he had passed to her in PEER. 'It fell out of your pocket when you fainted in the garage. You might want to put it on just so you don't, you know, lose it again.'

'Yes, of course,' Keix replied after a second's hesitation. She stood up and extended her hand towards Zej.

Instead of placing the pendant into her outstretched palm, Zej unclasped it and stepped towards her. The soapy piquant smell grew stronger when he looped both arms around her neck to fasten the hook.

Keix stiffened but made no protest. Now that her mind was a little clearer, she was reminded of the time she had received the necklace from her mother. It had been late at night on her eleventh birthday when her mum had sat her down and given her the trinket, enclosed in a small black velvet box. She had told Keix that it was a gift from her father and insisted on putting it on for her. She had even made Keix promise never to take it off.

Days after that exchange, her mum had gone in to work and never come back. Ghosts had attacked her workplace, which was located on the outskirts of Sector B. It had been reported in the news that Atros troopers had had to use the newly developed black hole rounds to curb this unprecedented attack, and that the bodies of those who had been caught within the firing range could never be retrieved.

When Keix had heard the announcement, she had thought of contacting her father. She had even taken out the card that had come with the necklace and read it again, even though she had the words memorized.

It is customary for us to gift our descendants with a family heirloom when they reach the age of eleven. The number has great significance in Kulcan culture. Perhaps one day you will find out why.

The thin and slanted handwriting, with each letter imprinted distinctly, revealed nothing. The words were just ink on a card. Without a number or return address or even a clue on how to contact him. Keix had later burned the card in the toilet. Come to think of it, she had never asked her mother if her dad had given the gift to her when he had left, or if the two of them had still been in contact all those years. She had never thought to figure out what her feelings for her father were. Her mother had had nothing but good things to say about him. In fact, Keix had always been secretly proud of her exceptional physical abilities, which she knew she had because she was half-Kulcan. But her mother had never spoken his name out loud. He was always 'your father'. He was not, and would probably never be, in her life. So she didn't think it mattered very much, growing up. Much less when her mother was dead.

Keix had been moved to an institution in the city centre where she had stayed until she was old enough to enrol herself into ATI at fourteen. She never took the necklace off to honour what she thought of as her mother's last wish. But she preferred to think of it as a gift from her mother instead.

Her voice trembling a little, Keix thanked Zej again. Just as he was straightening up after the necklace was secured, they heard a smattering of footsteps above.

Keix and Zej jumped back from each other just as Pod and a couple of people Keix didn't know stepped into the room.

Pod gave a dramatic groan and said, 'Please tell me we didn't just walk in on both of you kissing. I've been saying it for ages: Get a room. And your room is right there!' He gestured to the corridor and leaned his hip against the hologram table. His familiar, genuine smile was in place and he was wearing a pair of slightly oversized square spectacles that accentuated his long, friendly eyes and narrow nose. But his hair was now ash red and curly (it had been purple, short, straight and spiky the last time Keix saw him), his shoulders seemed broader and his arms bulkier.

Keix made a rude gesture at Pod. Admittedly, like the younger recruits later on, she had harboured a crush on Zej for a short while in her first year at ATI because of

how exceptionally cool and mature he seemed next to his
raucous friend. She had never told anyone about this lapse
in judgement, not even Vin. But Pod, as always, seemed to
have a knowing glint in his eyes every time he teased her
about being with Zej.

'Kissing? Your imagination's too tame. We were just—'
Keix said, then paused purposefully before adding, 'Well,
your naïve little mind wouldn't be able to deal with what we
were doing before you walked in. Right, Zej?'

At her outrageous confession, Zej gave a choked cough
while Pod laughed heartily.

'Glad to have you back, Keix,' Pod said. 'Glad to have
you back.'

He waved to the short and slender girl standing next to
him, who looked as aloof as he was affable, 'This is Maii.'

If not for the glint of amusement in her eyes, Maii
could have very well passed for a wax figurine. She was
dressed in black from head to toe—body-hugging leather
jacket, skinny jeans and knee-high, laced combat boots.
Her outfit was about as fierce as Pod's was casual, with his
dark jeans and black T-shirt, printed with a simple pattern
of lime green triangles across the chest. Maii's build,
piercing silver eyes and neon pink hair layered heavily at
the neck reminded Keix of Vin. A three-inch-long scar ran
from her right temple to the corner of her mouth; it gave
her a scheming and sinister look but it didn't detract from
the beauty of her high cheekbones and expressive eyes.

If the colour of Maii's hair hadn't been a giveaway that
she was Pod's Ifarl associate who had taken control of her
mind the moment she had left the underground prison, the

impersonal 'hey' she uttered following Pod's introduction would have confirmed it.

Keix would have recognized that dulcet voice anywhere.

'You might want to reconsider the hair colour. Doesn't really fit with the whole dominatrix vibe you've got there,' Keix's tone was sharp. She decided she was going to hold a grudge for not being able to run away from the Odats at PEER against Maii for the foreseeable future.

'Well, at least I'm not the one chained up,' Maii shot right back.

Keix tried to mask her surprise with anger as she held Maii's glare. Did she know about Vin? Or was the choice of words purely coincidental? Hastily, she buried her thoughts because she wasn't sure if Ifarls could read minds as well as control them.

Pod interrupted. 'Come now . . . there's no need for this type of hostility. We're *all* on the same side—yours, Keix,' he said, in the most conciliatory way he could manage.

'She almost got me caught,' Keix said, still looking at Maii.

'That was me, all right?' Pod said hurriedly. '*Huuuuuge* oversight on my part. I'll make it up to you.'

Keix turned her glare at Pod.

'Okay, okay,' Pod cleared his throat. 'Look, this is Rold. He helped me shut down the lasers,' he rushed on and ushered a shy-looking teenage boy forward. 'If not for him, you might have been toast.'

'Urm, hello,' Rold said. He had striking good looks and lustrous brown hair that grazed his collarbone, and was dressed as casually as Pod, in a grey T-shirt and faded jeans. His sharp eyes kept darting back and forth from Keix to his other teammates.

After a long silence, Keix addressed Rold, 'Thanks.'

'I just followed Pod's instructions,' Rold replied with a nervous and hesitant smile. 'He's the genius hacker.'

'Don't let him take all the credit. If his head gets any bigger, he won't be able to fit through the door,' Keix said, giving a smug Pod an annoyed glare.

'Anyway,' Zej interrupted, 'you must have a lot of questions.'

'*Really?*' Keix raised an eyebrow at him. It eased the strained atmosphere in the room a little. And it almost felt like the old times, this inside joke of theirs to state the obvious.

Rold turned his head to his shoulder and failed to suppress a grin. Even Maii gave a half-smile.

Questions fought their way to Keix's mouth and all she could do was stutter while trying to sort them out.

'But,' Zej continued, his expression turning serious, 'before we answer them, you should know that we're all working for a rebel organization.'

'WHAT?' Keix looked from Zej to Pod in utmost disbelief.

'That was succinct,' Pod muttered under his breath.

'What do you mean *you're* working for a rebel organization? I don't know about the two of them'—Keix pointed to Maii and Rold—'but *you* are an Atros soldier!' She whirled to face Pod. 'You too!'

'Well,' Pod said without a hint of distress, 'technically, yes. Until about a little over a month ago. I'm—' he paused, then gestured to Zej, '—we're still with Atros, but we're spying on them.'

'What? Why?' Keix exclaimed. Her mind was having trouble processing this new information. Against her choice, she was now involved with a rebel group—one that her friends, the people who had rescued her from PEER, were in. That was bound to put a damper on her mission to go about proving her innocence.

'Well, because you went missing!' Pod said, as if that explained everything.

Keix turned to Zej who said, 'It doesn't matter why and when I joined the rebel group.' He leaned back and clammed up to emphasize his point.

To avert the awkward silence that everyone could see coming from sectors away, Pod jumped in, 'Yeah, what matters now is we've got you out from PEER, and you're in a safe house in the middle of a patch of woods. Your body's been fed a lot of sedatives for the past two years. That's *a lot* of time, if you hadn't noticed. I, for one, am shocked that you can spin around and cast accusing looks at us now. Well, okay, not that shocked to tell the truth, with your Kulcan blood mojo and all. But the point is that you're going to need time to get your strength back. And this is the best place to do that.' He took Keix's absence of a retort as a positive sign, so he went on to recap what he had told her over the earpiece during her escape. As he explained, he drew up news and footages on the hologram table, adding timelines to help her establish a better picture of what had happened in these two years.

'Sector L was attacked by rebel troops last night,' announced a female newscaster, the face of the prime time Atros City News. 'It appears that the insurgents have managed to get their hands on the exclusive black hole bullets that Atros has developed . . .'

Sector L attacked by rebel troops: Close to thirty Atros soldiers perished or captured as hostages, wrote another prominent paper.

Conspiracists: Sector L attack was a cover-up, said an independent publication, notorious for its anti-Atros views.

'Three suspects have been brought in for questioning regarding the Sector L attacks last week,' said the same female reporter from before. 'A mass memorial will be held later this week for the fallen Atros soldiers, while authorities assure the public that investigations are ongoing . . .'

Something churned in the pit of Keix's stomach as Pod pulled up more headlines, almost all of them taking the same line of reporting. There was no mention that Atros suspected that spies were involved in the operation, nor of any paranormal activity, just as Pod had told her.

'Nothing adds up, right?' Pod asked after he had gone through all the information that he'd collected. He paused in consideration, then added, 'Except perhaps the conspiracy one—come to think of it now. I dug and dug. But everyone who was present at the incident was either dead or had been arrested. It wasn't like I could speak to them. I got—' he made a sound at the back of his throat '—zilch. Nothing. Until Zej came to me.'

'How did you know where I was?' Keix asked, turning to Zej once again.

'The rebel groups may be small and disorganized, but when something this major happens, we talk. To each other. Our agendas aren't all that different. And none of us—none that I know of—would ever carry out an op like this. What can we achieve? More ridicule? Or hate?' Zej asked. He was as serious as Keix had ever seen. From his tone, she gathered that he had been with the guerrilla group much longer than Pod. *All the time in Atros and I never realized it*, she thought to herself. *Maybe I never knew Zej that well, after all. Or did something drastic happen to make him change his views? Will I ever find out?*

Why are you so sure you haven't already found out? asked a snide voice inside Keix's head. Or are you ignoring the fact that Atros tortures its own troopers—like you—and hires Odats as guards in one of its most prestigious facilities?

Keix tried to shake off the growing sense of misgiving within her, one that she thought she had just quashed. 'So someone told you that I was imprisoned under PEER?' she asked Zej, sickened to the bone. Saying it out loud meant that she was, to some extent, accepting Zej's and Pod's stories.

Pod cleared his throat, while Rold tensed and stared at his sneakers as if he was afraid that they would run away. Maii's expression remained enigmatic. Zej, however, looked resolute as he took a deep breath and said, 'Not someone. I knew you were there because I processed the order.'

Keix's blood turned cold as the memories, still fresh in her mind from her recent dreams, reminded her of the pain she had gone through and how despondent she had felt after going through rounds and rounds of torture. 'What? What do you mean you *processed the order*? Like flipping burger patties?' Her voice had dropped so low that she was sure no one would have heard her if everyone in the room wasn't deathly quiet.

But Zej didn't flinch at the menace in her tone. He explained evenly, 'Months after Sector L was attacked, I was called into one of those sealed and unmarked rooms in PEER and asked to monitor the torture of someone who was suspected of being a traitor involved with the incident.'

'And you did it knowing it was me?' Keix wasn't aware of when or how it happened, but she was suddenly standing in front of Zej, her face inches from his. Her blood was coursing through her entire body, roaring in her ears especially.

Zej raised both his hands in surrender, but he stood his ground. Pod scooted to the far side of the table. Maii didn't move an inch. Rold, who had moved to a corner of the room when this conversation started, was staring wide-eyed at the scene in front of him.

'The room I was in only had monitors with graphs and numbers. You were held in a separate room because we're not allowed to know anything about our test subjects. Even if there was surveillance footage, I don't know where they keep it. I only managed to catch a glimpse of you because a guard happened to come out of the room you were in as I walked past.'

'But you continued to oversee the torture, even after knowing it was me?'

Zej shook his head. 'I didn't know if it was you I was doing the tests on every time I entered the monitoring room. They rotated the prisoners. It weighed on me, of course. But I had to maintain my cover so I could snoop around undetected. I couldn't find out where they were taking you, so I went to Pod.'

Pod nodded his head vigorously, 'When we finally tracked you down using a pattern of codes that I deciphered, you were already in forced hibernation in the SOUP—Sea of Unidentifiable Prisoners, I'm calling it, even though you might have been the only one in it. I'm not sure. Although, how important of a prisoner do you have to be to have such a huge cell, or cave, of your own, huh? Sorry, I got side-tracked. Where was I? Oh, I found you. Then we had to borrow some resources and formulate a plan to get you out. Luckily for you, I was on the team, so I guess you were only in the SOUP for about three months, from what I gather? The near-two years of torture notwithstanding. But, hey, we broke you out the first chance we got.'

Keix couldn't believe that Pod was spinning this into a simple search-and-rescue operation. The jumble of thoughts in her head was like a tangled ball of yarn. She simply couldn't find the energy to be entertained or exasperated by his chatter.

Instead of acknowledging him, she said the first thing that came to her mind, 'I need to see Oron. Where is he?' She wouldn't have thought that it was possible for the air in the room to become more still, but it did.

This time, it was Maii who spoke, her beautiful voice at total odds with the words that she uttered, 'Oron is dead.'

Keix's breathing became quick and shallow. *No, it can't be*, she told herself, pacing back and forth in front of the armchair. Her shirt was sticking to her back again and the starry sky that had repeatedly obscured her vision since her escape from PEER was threatening to engulf her once again.

Pod touched Keix's shoulder in a gesture of comfort. But she reacted reflexively, twisting his fingers and flipping him over her shoulder. He landed on the coffee table, splintering it. He rolled around, groaning in pain and hugging his arm tenderly.

Keix pushed her way out of the room as Rold rushed forward to help Pod up. She needed to reach the toilet before the contents of her stomach found their way to her mouth. As she started retching, she thought she heard Pod's shout through the corridor saying, 'Yep, I'm glad we got all the tough conversations out of the way first.'

5

The Night of Legends

'You really should stop trying to escape, you know?' a cheerful voice called out from behind Keix. 'It's such a waste of good effort.'

I have to get out of here, Keix told herself. She cast a quick glance over her shoulder and her heartbeat quickened. She kept running repeatedly into an invisible wall at the edge of the forest that concealed their safe house, which, from the outside, looked like a dilapidated single-storey hut.

The figure stalking her was already at the halfway point between her and the hut even though he was taking his time weaving through the clusters of thin and tall trees arranged like interlacing cages. Keix could see his grey T-shirt and faded jeans disappearing into the shadows before they reappeared again. But the constant soft crunching of his boots was a regular beat counting down the time he needed to close the distance between them.

Sunlight streaked through willowy branches and narrow leaves, creating a mesmerizing collage of dappled light on the forest floor. The mellow fragrance of the greenery permeated Keix's senses, almost sedating her, but she had worked herself into a full-blown panic mode.

In a last-ditch effort, she gritted her teeth and slammed her body into the imaginary barrier with all the strength she could muster. But it was useless; neither strength nor scheming could break the enchantment Maii had put on her.

Incensed, Keix recalled how Maii had unceremoniously stood outside the bathroom while she had been puking her guts out and said in that sing-song voice of hers, 'You will not leave the premises of this safehouse until I lift the charm'.

'What the hell is your problem?' Keix had shouted, standing up and wiping spit from her mouth. The alien strand of command had crawled its way into her mind and bound itself there. It was too late to resist the spell.

Standing behind Maii, Pod had appeared both reproachful and apologetic, 'You would run at the first opportunity. We're just trying to keep you safe.'

'I don't need protecting!' Keix shouted, and then immediately began coughing uncontrollably at the strain.

Pod's eyes narrowed. 'Yeah? Have you looked in the mirror at all? You're all skin and bones. You wouldn't stand a chance in a fight with me—hell, even Rookie Rold could hold his own against you right now. You'd still be trapped in SOUP if we hadn't gotten you out.'

Keix was angered by this reminder of her weakened state. But she knew that Pod was right. She then tried a different tack at the mention of her imprisonment. In a more reconciliatory tone, she said, 'How can you be so sure that I will be safe here? Trouble could come knocking and I won't be able to escape. Like what happened at PEER!'

To Keix's surprise, Maii was the one who replied. 'I'm not as careless as Pod. Nor as confident that this place will not be discovered. So you will not be able to go beyond the forest clearing outside of this safehouse, until I lift the charm. Unless you're in danger.'

Even though she barely knew Maii, she had had a feeling that this was the best compromise she could get from her. To tell the truth, she felt a reluctant respect for Maii despite her abrasive attitude. Also, she didn't think she should leave this place until she figured out what her next move should be. The pieces on the chessboard had all been scattered randomly; she needed to strategize and come up with a new approach to deal with her situation.

As her pursuer neared, Keix lay on the ground, resigned. This 'unless you're in danger' clause hadn't turned out to be the potential loophole she thought it would be. Either that, or she hadn't found a way to exploit it.

After almost a month of recuperation, Keix had begun to feel more like her old self. Pod had kept calling it 'the Kulcan mojo' until it annoyed Maii so much she told him to stop. Forcefully. Incontrovertibly. Keix had to choke back her laughter at Pod's outrage.

The change wasn't just physical. In a way, the hut had started to feel like home too. The four of them—Pod, Maii, Rold and herself—had developed a casual camaraderie. Zej, in the meantime, had kept out of her way after his huge revelation. He knew her well enough to let her have some space to sort out her feelings about his betrayal. He dropped by a couple of times but only stayed long enough to update everyone about what was going on; it was business as usual for Atros. Atros was covering up Keix's escape under the guise of a drill. Other than that, Zej never revealed any of the rebel group's plans, if there were any at all. Keix was still getting her information on a strictly need-to-know basis.

This morning, Maii and Pod had left the safe house to replenish their supplies. So Keix had thought she might try her luck and test the boundaries of Maii's charm since she was going to be left alone with Rold.

As he came up to her, she reflected on the fact that Rold was easily the nicest person she had ever met. There was no way she could convince her subconscious that he posed any danger to her life.

Keix sat up and shrugged. 'I had to try,' she replied and took Rold's outstretched hand.

Rold laughed. 'One of the few things Zej and Pod said about you that isn't wrong.'

The corner of Keix's mouth turned up in amusement. After Rold had got over his initial shyness, he had confessed, abashed, 'From the stories Pod told me, I thought you were demented and ferocious. My instincts, and the fact that Zej seemed utterly entertained by the stories, told me he was exaggerating, since no one would be mad enough to break a person like that out from PEER. But you never know with Pod,' he laughed. 'He was, er, very convincing. Also, PEER seemed impenetrable—to me, at least. Not Pod. I've never seen anyone work through a system like him.' It was apparent that Rold held Pod in high esteem from the slight tilt of his head whenever he talked about him.

'Anyway, now that you've tried, and failed, maybe we can continue with our training?' Rold proposed.

The day after her confrontation with Maii, Rold had asked Keix if she was interested in training him to fight. Keix had been reluctant, but she had agreed, thinking it might speed up her recovery. It took the edge off being cooped up in the hut, and the workout dispatched each day with a disquieting efficiency. On their first day of training, Pod had announced loftily, '*I* am the master of your master.' He pointed to Keix and added, 'You will only be eligible to spar with me when you can defeat her.'

Maii had narrowed her eyes at that. But every night since then, she had walked with the three of them—Keix, Rold and Pod—to a clearing at the edge of the forest and quietly watched Keix and Rold training on the sidelines with Pod as the clouds and winking stars made their way across the sky.

Keix and Rold's training had fallen into a comfortable rhythm after a couple of days. He would attempt to pin her to the ground, and she would counter his moves. After a set, she would tell him what he was or wasn't doing right and suggest ideas to improve his manoeuvres. Then, she would go on the offensive while he tried to defend himself.

Although Rold hadn't won a match since their first one (she had had to call timeout and sit down to right her spinning head after running through a series of standard attacking and defensive stances with him), he was improving at an impressive rate. He had a keen eye and was a natural at spotting Keix's staged tells and guessing her next move.

Today's training was no different. Rold grunted as Keix's kick felled him once again. 'You have an unfair advantage,' he grumbled, rubbing his offended behind.

'You told me not to hold back. And you tend to hesitate before you lunge at me. Remember: a split second makes all the difference. Listen to your instincts and trust your body,' Keix said, shaking her recently cut fringe out of her eyes. Her long, lifeless hair reminded her of the time she spent in the SOUP every time she saw her reflection, so she had sheared it back into the chin-length bob she preferred. The imprisonment had taken a toll on her. She still felt faint every time she exerted herself, but she had seen a marked improvement in the past week.

'Hey,' said Rold, waving his hand in front of Keix, 'are you having an episode again?' That was what Rold called her near-fainting spells.

'Oh!' exclaimed Keix, snapping out of her thoughts. 'No. No, I think my body's over that.'

'You sure? Your eyes were glazed over,' Rold continued, looking concerned.

'Yes, I'm sure.' Keix plonked herself down, signalling an end to the training.

Rold shrugged and sat down next to her in companionable silence. If Keix's calculations were right, it would be a few minutes before the first pinkish-purple streaks of sunset appeared in the sky. This was fast becoming her favourite time of the day. She found that she liked this sun. It didn't have as strong an intensity as the scorching afternoon sun, and wasn't as cheery as its rising counterpart. And there was just enough time—several minutes, not too long nor short—for her to soak in the sun's balanced energy before its mood soured and it became a jaded setting sun.

Even the qiues—birds the size of her pinkie—that twittered all day long would line up on the highest branches and still their electric green feathers and thin red beaks to observe this sight.

As she sat there, looking at the sky, Keix realized she had never thought of herself as someone who enjoyed peacefulness. To her, the word had always been just another way of saying 'boring'. She had always been a thrill seeker at heart and Vin's partner-in-crime. Other trainees in Atros had referred to both of them as the Troublemaker Twins, a term not unlike the Dashing Duo. The differences between them and Zej and Pod were that for one, they hadn't coined the term themselves; and two, they had never warmed up to the moniker enough to use it to refer to their friendship.

Basking in the quiet moment, Keix questioned if she had really known true peace at all.

'Oka,' Rold said, breaking the silence. 'That's what we call ourselves. Oka. Did Zej tell you that?'

Keix shook her head. Several times, she felt like asking Pod about this rebel group that he and Zej had joined. When and why had they become involved with them? How big were they? How did they operate? Surely Atros would have taken action if the insurgents had gained so much ground as to plant spies within their ranks or convert their soldiers?

But the questions died once they reached her tongue. The more she knew about them, the less easy it would be for her to claim non-involvement. Besides, she was still trying to decide how she would feel if Atros took her back and she had to rat on the people who had rescued her in the first place. Although she had to admit that the chances of her being allowed to rejoin Atros were probably as slim as Pod developing a sense of humility.

So all Keix had been doing was reading and watching the mainstream news on the control table, which was still located in the basement with the wrecked coffee table. There, in that dusty armchair, she found herself turning into a conspiracy theorist, analysing, over and over again, every single word in the feed.

Piecing them together with her recent discoveries, she couldn't help but agree with Pod that the stories didn't add up. Talk about being paranoid. It was a slippery downward spiral.

Shaking herself out of her own musings, Keix saw that Rold was still silent. He didn't seem to be in a hurry to continue his revelations, so Keix thought harder. The word stirred up a distant memory of a conversation she had with Vin.

Keix paused, the definition of the word tingling at the tip of her tongue. 'It's . . . an extinct nocturnal creature that the Ifarls worship?' This was probably the only thing she knew about this strange race, other than the fact that they could communicate with mindspeak and manipulate other people's actions.

Rold quirked an eyebrow, then made a diagonal bobbing motion with his head. 'Not wrong, but not exactly right. I'm impressed you know this much, actually.'

Keix gave him the side-eye.

'Do you know when ghost sightings began to increase exponentially?' Rold asked.

'Seventy years ago,' Keix replied with confidence.

'Seventy-*two*,' Rold corrected. 'Do you know why or how it happened?'

Keix imitated Rold's head-bobbing action. 'No one knows. There are theories, but the most feasible one was that there was a build-up in paranormal energies in our world, and in theirs, and then—'Keix brought her clenched fists together then opened and pulled them apart quickly, 'boom—one happy family.'

'Not wrong—'

'—but not exactly right,' Keix interrupted.

Rold grinned at her.

'Have you heard of the Ifarl rhyme, "The Night of Legends"?' he continued.

'Oh, are we quizzing each other now?' Keix asked mockingly. 'Well, if that's the case, I have one for you. Have you come across a tome entitled *Ifarl History and their Rhymes: An Encyclopaedia*? Because I would love to read it. In case *you* haven't heard, the Ifarls aren't really into oversharing.'

Both of them laughed, before dropping off into silence.

Rold took a slow deep breath and exhaled with his eyes closed and his lips twisted to the side. Somehow, Keix knew that he was searching inwardly for reassurance to continue the conversation.

'"The Night of Legends" is an ancient Ifarl rhyme,' Rold explained, before reciting it in a deliberate manner.

Nine of Stars,
Cut sky's bars.
Traces line,
Make ties bind.
Bae born,
Mae worn.
Bae be bound, powers—unbound.

Evil dwells,
Where fear swells.
Evil thrills,
Where joy fills.
Teach right,
Tread light.
Bae be born, of Nine Stars bond.

A long, ponderous silence fell as both of them contemplated the same words in different ways. Keix thought the words 'bae' and 'mae' might mean 'baby' and 'mother' in the Ifarl language, but she couldn't be sure. And she had never in her life come across any stories that told of nine stars in the sky, so she wasn't sure what to make of the rhyme.

Rold broke the silence in a sombre voice, his eyes fixed on the smooth green bark of a nearby tree as if he were reading words off it that only he could see.

'The Ifarls fear nothing more than that which is unknown to them. In their lore, the nine dimmest stars in the sky represent the unknown. It is said that once every millennium, when these nine stars line up in a straight line and divide the sky into exact halves, a riddle will be passed down in the form of a newborn child for them to solve. A test of sorts.

'This child is born at the exact moment these stars align. This bond allows the child to inherit the limitless power of these stars combined, but it also kills the mother,' Rold explained.

'That's pretty dark,' Keix said.

Rold nodded. 'Ninety-three years ago, an Ifarl boy was born on this prophesized night, when the nine stars lined up and shone brighter than they usually did in the cloudless sky. His mother died right after delivering him, without so much as a gasp or sigh. The Ifarl elders took him under their wing to study him, and they named him Iv't, an ancient Ifarl word for void.

'Despite the ominous rhyme and the elders' reservations, Iv't grew up to become the pride of the Ifarls. He had an abstract way of thinking that came with his powers, and they all agreed that they had more to learn than to fear from him.'

Keix was listening with rapt attention. The qiues had resumed chirping long ago, singing a curious tune, almost an accompaniment to Rold's words. The sky had turned a blazing orange, and Keix could feel a sudden chill in her bones as the temperature in the surrounding air dipped more than it normally did around this time of the day.

Keix was reminded of how her mother would sit down with her before bedtime to read fairy tales to her when she was young. She used to wonder if the Kulcan had their own tales, and if things would be different if her father had stayed with this family of his. Would he be the one reading to her? But it had never once crossed her mind to ask about the Ifarls' version of folk stories. The familiarity and candour with which Rold told her this—not to mention how unusual it was that he knew this at all—made it far more intriguing than she could ever imagine.

Numbness was creeping into the tips of her toes, so Keix drew up her legs and tucked them under her, watching Rold, who continued to speak with a faraway look in his eyes.

'Years later, Iv't married a human girl, whom he had fallen in love with, against the elders' advice. Ifarls frown upon mixed unions, especially for someone like Iv't, who they thought had great potential. The newly-weds moved to the edge of the Ifarl forest, away from the secretive community, out of respect for his people, and lived in seclusion for a while.

'A few months after Iv't and his wife welcomed their firstborn, he received an urgent summons to attend the Ifarl council. It turned out to be a trap. When Iv't returned to his hut, his wife's dead body was almost cold and his only daughter was missing.

'The Ifarls claimed that they had not summoned him and in his grief and anxiety to find answers, Iv't reached, as deep as he could, into his bottomless well of power, and opened a portal to the ghost realm in search of his wife.'

'Did he find her?' Keix interjected.

Rold nodded.

Keix's gut knew what he would say before he opened his mouth, although a small part of her held out hope that he wouldn't utter the words.

Rold looked into Keix's eyes, and she mouthed the words at the same time as he said them out loud, 'But she was different.'

Keix shuddered. Suddenly, her ears seemed attuned to every single sound around her, including the muted vibration of the air. It was as if her hearing had been obstructed by invisible ear plugs all her life.

Rold's voice came through exceptionally sharp and crisp when he said, 'His wife's ghost clung on to him so she could absorb his life energy, draw power from him. The agony drove Iv't mad despite his power. But he used his last bit of sanity to curse those who had destroyed his family. And because he hadn't seen the ghost of his daughter, he held out hope that she was still alive. He couldn't see the faces of the people who had attacked and killed his wife in the memories that she was unwittingly feeding him, but he thought he saw the image of some creatures, wild, hairy, four-legged creatures, carrying away a small bundle. So he gathered the last of his power and cast a spell of protection upon those he assumed had saved his daughter's life; it would protect them against this onslaught of ghosts that he was unleashing upon the world.'

'He didn't close the portal,' Keix said flatly. A surreal feeling settled in the centre of her being. What Rold was telling her was one of those fables that made sense when you first heard it; and would continue to sound even more logical during subsequent retellings.

Rold nodded. He looked exhausted and, for a moment, much older.

'And the creatures . . . they were okas?' Keix asked, thinking back to how this conversation had begun.

It was dark now. What little they could see of the hut before the sunset had disappeared into the background, giving the impression that both of them were stranded in the darkness.

Her eyes lingered on the slight sheen of sweat on Rold's forehead and nose, and the two glittering dots of his eyes that were visible in the dim starlight without really seeing them.

Rold gave another nod.

Keix's hands were clammy and she felt an itch at a spot on the back of her neck. Her mind had entered a frenzied state and her instincts were telling her that the story that Rold was relating was real, even though she didn't want to believe it because the story had struck a chord of fear in her that she had never felt before. So she tried to sound derisive as she said, 'Is that why you guys named yourselves after them? Because you think it symbolizes some saviour in some old story or rhyme? Has anyone even seen an oka? It could just be something that the storyteller made up to mess with people's minds.'

But Rold only gave a short laugh. 'You can't bring yourself to admit that a part of you thinks that the story is true. Just as you can't bring yourself to admit that Atros betrayed you, despite all the evidence right under your nose.'

Keix didn't want to address the second part of Rold's accusation. Instead, she said, 'No, I *know* it's just some crackpot story they tell you to get you to enrol into a rebel group. But I do give due credit to the one who made it up. It's a good story.'

That struck a nerve. In an instant, Rold's amiable smile vanished and his voice took on a hard edge. 'Okas are not unlike the extinct wolves in human myths—they're *real*. And it isn't some made-up story. My great-grandfather married Iv't's daughter.'

'I'm sorry—what?' Keix's shock made her forget to appear sceptical. Rold had Ifarl ancestry too? Keix resisted the urge to part his hair to see if he had markings on his scalp like Vin. Instead, she hid her astonishment with more sarcasm. 'So now you're telling me that you're *rebel royalty*? Or that you only believe in that story because your great-grandfather set up this sorry excuse for a rebel group to bring down Atros?'

Rold stood up and brushed the soil off his butt. His tone was edged with contempt when he replied, 'The Ifarls have nothing to do with Oka; they wouldn't bother themselves with something as trivial as trying to take down Atros.'

'Then why are you with them?'

'The Ifarls despise anyone who is not pure. They guard their secrets too closely to risk having an outsider like me in their midst.'

'Is that why Maii is with you? She's mixed too?'

'No. Maii is a full Ifarl,' replied Rold before turning his back on Keix.

'You're not answering my question,' said Keix to his retreating back.

As she watched Rold disappear through the doorway of the hut, she thought about his bitter tone. Her treasonous heart thundered as she stood in the darkness and slowly let her breath out. She realized that the qiues had switched to singing a low, rumbling song, which was rather uncharacteristic of them. The stars gleamed like watchful eyes high in the sky, trying to determine her tentative mood.

The wind picked up a fraction, and a soft rustling came from the far end of the woods. The hair on the back of Keix's neck prickled, her Kulcan senses issuing a sure warning of some unseen danger.

Keix rushed towards the safe house to see that Rold was already halfway out of the door again. He had switched off all the lights in the house, but she could just about make out a sliver of light from under the trapdoor to the hidden basement.

Rold gestured for Keix to keep quiet as he walked up to her.

He leaned his head close to hers and whispered in her ear, 'There's a disturbance north of the barrier Maii put up. I've sent a message to the rest. I'll go check it out. Hide in the basement and wait for someone to reply.'

'No, I'll go with you. I can watch your back,' Keix insisted.

'No, you'll do as I say. If there's danger, remember Maii's words. Leave the safe house.'

Keix was shocked to feel the tingling thread of command of an Ifarl's spell worm its way into her brain at Rold's words. His charm felt different from her past encounters with other Ifarls, like Maii and Vin, but she couldn't pinpoint how. Her resentment surged as her body jumped to obey his words. When she reached the basement of the hut, she could see, through the fuzzy surveillance feed from the control table, Rold muttering and waving both arms, straight in a high arc towards the direction of the hut.

Keix didn't know what he was doing, but he slumped forward after that, as if the effort of doing it had exhausted him.

A split second later, a group of soldiers dressed in green-brown Atros trooper suits appeared out of nowhere and surrounded him. There were more than forty of them, and they advanced towards Rold, who staggered back with great difficulty.

'Where is Keix?' one of the soldiers asked.

Keix couldn't tell who was speaking because they were all wearing helmets with tinted visors.

Rold's reply was a mocking laugh. Despite being cornered, there was no fear or hesitation in him.

This angered one of the soldiers, the tallest of the bunch. He stepped forward and, without warning, raised a gun and fired at Rold. In an instant, Rold was thrown back, landing sprawled on his back. His body began to spasm, his arms and legs locked rigidly to his side.

Keix's eyes widened in horror as foam spilled out of his open mouth. His body continued to jerk uncontrollably until it came to a standstill and a glow enveloped his body. The bluish glow seemed to emit from within Rold.

Keix was transfixed by the screen. She jumped when Maii's voice came over softly through the control table, 'Rold, hold on. We're ten—'

Before Maii could finish her sentence, the static cut her out and the entire basement was plunged into absolute darkness.

6

Acquisition

Keix backed up against a corner of the basement. The darkness was so complete that she couldn't see her fingers despite the fact that she was pressing the back of her palms hard against her lips, stifling a scream. Whether it was one of horror or frustration, she couldn't tell.

The cool air stung her nose with each measured breath she took. Her ears strained to pick up the smallest disruption in the air over the sound of the relentless torrent of blood surging through them.

After a long tense silence, a faint buzz came from the stairs. As her body tensed for a fight, the lights suddenly came back on and the monitor on the control table flickered back to life. The forty-odd soldiers she had seen earlier were milling about in front of the hut. Rold was nowhere to be seen, so why were the troopers still looking around instead of descending upon the house? Surely any type of trap would have already been triggered, what with the way they were sweeping every inch of the land.

Keix's gaze was glued to the screen. Her stillness belied the raging turmoil within. To all outward appearances, these were Atros soldiers; from the way they coordinated the search, right down to their bootlaces. Yet the viciousness of that soldier who had shot Rold—his casual disregard for the potential consequences of his action . . . Keix shook her head, as if that could shake off the feeling of dread creeping over her.

It was easy to spot the shooter in the crowd even though every one of them wore a helmet. His height and self-assured swagger set him apart from the rest, making him seem like the natural leader of the group. Keix focused her wrath on him. She wished she knew who exactly he was and who had sanctioned him to carry out the hit.

He paused in mid-stride, as if he had felt her glare. Then he turned around and walked towards the camera. His black helmet grew in size on the control screen until the monitor was completely black. Keix inhaled sharply when he flipped his visor up to reveal a pair of yellow eyes that glowed with a level of intensity that bordered on the deranged.

Keix gulped down an unnecessary breath of air. It wasn't just that the trigger-happy trooper's eyes seemed to see right past the lens of the camera into her—it was also that they were simply another item added to the ever-growing list of things that she had never seen before, reminding her that she was in a different world from her pre-SOUP days.

Now, she was stuck in a basement with nowhere to run. Over three dozen trained soldiers would soon discover that she was unarmed and trapped in an underground room. They had twice the number of people Keix was confident she could take out. Out of danger? Keix sniffed; if she failed to beat them, it would be an understatement to say that Rold had seriously miscalculated her odds. At the thought of him, Keix felt as if her heart was being squeezed. An image of her own dark brown eyes, glowing gold and crazed appeared in her mind for no discernible reason. She thrust it away hastily. She had to focus.

Keix surveyed the dingy place, trying to strategize how best to conduct her mini battle while directing the camera to follow Crazy Eyes. As the camera swivelled round, something irregular on the screen made her pause. The hut's patio had . . . disappeared? Her jaw dropped.

Was that what Rold had been doing when he had 'waved' his arms at the hut? *He was concealing it?* Keix gaped. She had never heard of such power. *But you had never heard of 'The Night of Legends' either, had you?* a voice in her head asked. *And a great deal of other things, no?*

Keix sighed. There were times when she felt she was a victim of her own snarky personality. It used to be funny; now, it wasn't.

She waited in silence as she watched Crazy Eyes return unerringly to the exact spot in front of the camera and gave it—her?—a snide smile. Keix's pulse quickened. He must know about Rold's enchantment! But how?

Then, he turned and shouted a command. With a wave of his hand, the troopers gathered into neat rows and filed out of the space. After what felt like ages later, when Keix felt the strain from Rold's command lift from her mind, she knew that she could finally leave the basement. Yet, there was a nagging feeling at the back of Keix's mind. Crazy Eyes wouldn't be the sort to give up easily. She was sure that he had a Plan B, a Plan C, plans all the way up to the letter Z. It was likely he was somewhere in the vicinity—far enough to make her feel safe, but near enough to still reach her—setting a trap for her. But between staying here in the basement and taking her chances out in the open, there was no way she would choose the former. And who knew how much longer it would take Pod and Maii to get back?

Keix gasped. Pod and Maii! They could be walking into Crazy Eyes's trap at that very minute. Even if she had wanted—perhaps still wanted—to escape from their house arrest, she owed them the decency of at least giving them a warning.

As soon as Keix stepped out of the basement, it disappeared. She found herself in complete darkness again. It was as if she was buried alive, except the earth wasn't pressing in on her. She stretched out her arms, unsure of what she was feeling for. Her fingers touched something solid and smooth. A wall? She shuffled her feet and had to stifle a yelp when a sharp pain shot through her toe—she had kicked something hard. As she pitched forward, she reflexively threw out her arms and felt her hand come into contact with something cool and cylindrical. *A handrail! Right. I must have kicked the bottom step of the stairs, which means I'm still in the hut, except I can't see it now*, thought Keix. She tried to use her memories of the hut's layout to test her theory.

Several misplaced steps, bumps and curses later, her head emerged from the ground and her lungs swelled with fresh air, soothing her frayed nerves slightly. She took care to ensure that she continued to count her steps until it felt like her feet were on level ground. She felt a weird hiss on her skin at the same moment, which she interpreted as a signal to indicate that the hut had vanished completely. She had a feeling that the change was permanent; even if she located the exact spot where the invisible stairs were, she would not be able to go back down again.

The stars that had been present in the sky when she and Rold had been having their heart-to-heart, had gone into hiding. Only a lone one remained, peeking out from behind a muggy grey cloud.

Keix stood still for a moment, trying to digest her new discoveries. Her musings were cut short by a distant gunshot that reverberated through the willowy trees. A sense of urgency seized Keix. Was it Crazy Eyes or Maii? She wasn't going to stay to find out.

Ignoring the pang of guilt she felt when she thought of Rold, she took off in what she assumed was the direction of the gunshot.

Keix skidded to a stop. The soles of her shoes made a crunching sound on the thin layer of gravel atop the soft soil of the forest, but she was glad that it wasn't distinctive or loud. She couldn't pinpoint exactly how long she had been running except that her legs were beginning to strain slightly.

She was lost. This was the fourth time she had circled back to this area. She could tell that it was the same cluster of trees, distinguished by their stick-thin trunks and leafless branches. Keix looked up at the murky sky. Even the last surviving star had winked out disappointingly. Now, there was practically no way to tell which direction she was heading.

Keix narrowed her eyes. She was certain that she had been moving in a straight line. There was no way she could have circled back. She cast another look around. There was a hint of a soft bluish glow from over the horizon. Was dawn approaching? Keix couldn't be sure. But her Kulcan senses were screaming at her to be careful. The air was devoid of the usual murmurs of the forest's inhabitants.

Just as that thought crossed her mind, she heard soft, rapid tapping like the footfalls of someone running near.

Without a second thought, Keix ran. She hadn't gotten very far when a silhouette slithered out from behind a tree; and that tree trunk definitely did not look wide enough to have concealed him. Keix leapt away from the figure as she felt a prickling sensation at the back of her neck.

There was something familiar about the man. Keix swallowed a gasp as he took a step forward. It was one of the Atros soldiers from the hut, and he was not wearing his helmet any more. A flare of anger replaced her shock when she realized it was Crazy Eyes. The strength of the emotion made her stand her ground instead of turning on her heel—which was what she thought she really ought to have done. She raised her clenched fists in front of her, ready for a fight.

The dim light gave a greyish pallor to the killer's face. It should have neutralized the intensity of his yellow eyes but instead, merely made them seem to glow more brightly.

Crazy Eyes's mouth twisted into a cruel smile. He raised a gun and fired.

Keix leapt aside a split second before the gun went off. She thanked her sharp instincts as she felt the bullet brush past her right fist. Dropping into a ball, she rolled to her side using her shoulder as a pivot. When she landed steadily in a crouch after the tumble, she snarled at the thin streak of red appearing on her knuckle.

A sedative, thought Keix, when numbness radiated out through her muscles from the bullet's graze. And a strong drug at that.

Another bullet whizzed past her cheek just as she whipped her head to the side. This time around, it was a hair's breadth from drawing blood. Adrenaline rushed through her veins like water from a broken dam, rendering the trace of sedative, which had found its way into her body, useless.

Crazy Eyes continued firing at her, barely missing his mark—he was a sharp-shooter, Keix would give him that, but she was better. She ran to a tree and kick-stepped against it, using the momentum to launch herself into a diagonal body spin at Crazy Eyes.

Bang! Another shot rang out as Keix flew towards Crazy Eyes. The next moment, she was reaching out with both hands—bang!—one grabbing on to the gun muzzle, the other tightening around his thumb and twisting it outwards, making him lose his grip on the gun, before landing on both feet without so much as a tiny sidestep. She turned the gun on the trooper and squeezed the trigger. Damn, he'd emptied the clip! She threw the gun to the side just as he lunged at her, ramming into her shoulders.

Keix bit back a cry at the contact and turned to face Crazy Eyes. He had lost the element of surprise. The two of them were now circling each other. Like shihs, the ferocious and graceful historic animals who fought to death, Keix decided that only one of them would leave this forest alive.

'Ah,' Crazy Eyes exclaimed, 'the legendary Kulcan speed, I see. I must say, I'm impressed.' He was even taller up close, looming at least a head over Keix. He spoke slowly and seemed to relish hissing out his Ss, extending them a tad longer than required; it was a sharp contrast to his gravelly voice, and the effect would have been intimidating for anyone, but not Keix because she had established the fact that she could move faster than him—a distinct advantage for her.

'Who are you?' Keix asked. Her tone was light, striving for an air of nonchalance, but her fists, clenched at her sides, and tense shoulders gave her away.

Crazy, on the other hand, was still swaggering, his thin lips curled into a cunning smile with corners as sharp as razors.

'I forget my manners,' he answered, like he had not just attempted to put ten rounds of hard-hitting sedative into her. 'I am Seyfer, overall commander of the Acquisitions team at *Atros*.'

Keix's eyebrows snapped together; she couldn't stop the reaction and she saw Seyfer's smirk widen.

He placed his right palm over his chest then raised it up in the organization's standard salute before twirling it in front of him and bowing down mockingly. It was the lowest form of insult in Atros culture, an insinuation that the person in front of you was so harmless that you'd expose your nape to him, all defences down.

Keix should have bristled at the gesture but she chose to seize the opportunity to aim a kick at his exposed neck. Her delivery would have been true if it had been an ordinary person she was attacking, but Seyfer was not fooled. With a speed Keix never saw coming, he grabbed the heel of her boot and pulled it upwards as he straightened up, toppling her onto her back with a loud thud. He pounced on her in an instant, pinning her wrists down to the sides of her face, his knee pressing down sharply on her chest.

Keix had underestimated him. As good as Seyfer was with guns, he was at least ten times better at hand-to-hand combat.

'What does Atros want with me?' Keix choked out the words. The pressure on her chest was making it hard to breathe. There was barely enough wiggle room for her to regain a fighting advantage over him. The glow from the horizon was drawing closer, but she felt nothing but the chill in her bones. Somehow, she knew that the light was not going to be her salvation.

'You're a prisoner. You escaped. Now you have to come back.'

Keix could hear the distinct menace in Seyfer's simplistic summary, even though his face betrayed none of the impatience she knew he was feeling.

'I was a trooper. And I was never disloyal to Atros.'

'Until you were,' Seyfer said, as if to conclude the conversation.

'Until Atros decided to torture me!' the words scraped at her already-dry throat like sandpaper.

'For information about your little rebel group.'

'I wasn't with them!'

'Hm . . . "wasn't" . . . does that mean you've changed your mind now? Tell me, how did your friends know where you were? And to rescue you the day before you were scheduled for your . . .' he pretended to search for the word, '*sentence*? Tsk, tsk, tsk. I'm curious.'

Keix pressed her lips together. She could tell that Seyfer wasn't interested in what she had to say. And the fact that he was literally spitting saliva all over her face with his hissing did not help improve her mood.

'What have I done wrong?'

'Wrong?' Seyfer chuckled. The sound proved even more grating than his studied nonchalance. 'No . . .' he shook his head, 'You haven't done anything wrong. Why would you ask that?'

'Then why am I a prisoner?'

'Your potential. It's not what you've done, but what you *can* do.'

Keix looked confused.

Seyfer continued in his crazed tone, 'You have no idea, do you? There, there. Why don't you come back with me? Willingly. The things we could do . . . after we get the first test over and done with.'

Keix put all her strength into trying to squirm sideways to throw Seyfer off. Her vision was getting blurrier by the second and she could taste bile. But she knew it was useless. After this show of rebellion, she let her body go limp as if in surrender.

'All right,' she cried. 'I want to know. Get off me and I'll go with you. Willingly.'

'Not putting up a fight? Tsk, tsk. You don't think I'd believe that, do you, darling *Kulcan*?' Seyfer tut-tutted disapprovingly, infusing barrels of acid into the last word. He took a deliberate pause, then continued, 'So you wouldn't mind if I cuff you, then?'

'Why not?' Keix said with the cheeriest smile she could manage.

Seyfer's eyes widened a fraction at her easy acquiescence; he had probably expected her to veto his suggestion so she could trap him into lowering his guard and escaping. But he recovered without missing a beat, bringing both her wrists together so he could secure them with one hand while he reached back into his waistband for his cuffs with the other.

Big mistake.

Keix looped the fingers of both her hands together and brought them down on Seyfer's head, hitting the side of his temple with a cracking sound. The distraction gave her enough leeway to twist to her side and roll out from under him.

She got to her feet and readied to attack Seyfer, who had fallen to his side clutching his forehead, when she felt something hard pressed to her back.

'Freeze,' a voice said, with the smallest hint of hesitation.

Keix froze. And she didn't try to hide the smile that came to her lips.

'Captain Sey—' the guard who was holding her captive addressed his leader. He never got to finish his sentence.

As the words left his lips, Keix had turned around, grabbed his wrists, flipped him on his back and fired the sedative gun at him before Seyfer could get to his feet.

The guard lay on the ground, motionless.

'Numbskull,' Keix murmured. She trained the gun on Seyfer, who was getting to his feet. She debated whether she should shoot him or try to get more information, cryptic as it was, out of him.

'Good feint. Very good,' Seyfer said with a mirthless laugh. 'But you shouldn't have done that.'

Keix glared at him. She could hear a chorus of shuffling feet hastening in their direction. Seyfer's troop must have caught up. Escape didn't look possible, but she refused to roll over and surrender. So she decided to try a different tack and get him to continue talking. That way, if she came out of this fight alive, she would at least have a little more information or an ace up her sleeve. She cast her mind back to one of the less cryptic things he had said before.

'What test are you talking about? I underwent the entire enchilada of standard tests at Atros when I enrolled as a trooper,' Keix asked.

She had hoped that feigning ignorance would stoke Seyfer's arrogance and make him slip up. But he was too smart to fall for it.

'Well, let's just say things have changed. For you,' he said, proving once again that he was the nonpareil of speaking obtusely. The footsteps were getting louder. And the glow, which Keix had thought had been coming from the rising sun, was reaching her through the trees instead of spreading through the skies. She tightened her grip on the gun, her knuckles whitening, knowing that that could only mean one thing: ghosts.

'I wish things were easier. That you'd make it easier for me,' Seyfer sighed as he dusted off his uniform fastidiously. 'I do abhor changes in my plans, you know. And the plan was to take you back to the Institute for testing. But I guess I'll have to improvise now.' He clapped his hands. The sound echoed in a low rumble to join the footsteps of figures who were moving out in unison from the shadows cast by the eerie glow of the spirits. Keix was doing a quick count of the number of guards when the light rushed towards her without a sound. The next thing she knew, pain was splitting through her entire body. Her head spun. Then it stopped as abruptly as it started.

Keix was on her back, her wrists and feet bound to whatever it was that she was lying on. A bright fluorescent light shone over her, blinding her. The pain had dulled. Her extremities were twitching uncontrollably.

Am I back in one of my memories?

Blurry shadows moved in and out of her view. The light, combined with her weak vision, produced halos around the shadows.

'Trial 65. Repeat voltage. Total time: Five minutes and three seconds,' announced a distant voice.

Immediately, even sharper pain seized Keix as her back arched up high and crashed back down. She was sure she would have flailed her arms if they hadn't been bound. An acrid smell filled her nose. There was a gag biting into the corners of her lips. She would have smiled at its redundancy.

She didn't think she could have managed a whimper, much less a scream.

The scene shifted.

Now, debilitating fear was flooding through her. Again, she was bound, this time upright, to a rectangular plank facing a curved silvery door. The door slid to the side with a hiss and the plank brought her forward into a cylindrical space. She tried to struggle but her body remained limp; she couldn't move even a finger. A masculine voice echoed softly in her ear. 'No . . . No . . .' it repeated, slurring a word as simple as this. Light appeared in a vertical line on the cylinder wall. It widened, then rushed at her, blinding her and sending pain ricocheting through her body—again.

Her visions mashed together. Blinding light. Whirring darkness. Pain. Fear. These scenes intercut each other, dancing to the low rumble of the man's words.

'No . . .' the man repeated. This time, it seemed different. Even though it sounded like it came from further away, it felt more tangible than it had before.

Then, just like when she fought the Odat back at PEER, a spark of power appeared at the back of her head. But instead of fizzling out, it grew in size and soon filled Keix with a mellow warmth that radiated throughout her body.

Keix's vision cleared. The cylinder was gone and she was back in the forest. The light rushing towards her was no longer a light, but a man with the ugliest sneer on his face. Half of his clothes had burned away, revealing charred skin that looked like it was still smoking. She struck out a reflexive punch at the burnt man. When her knuckle connected with his cheek, he turned into a bunch of lights that scattered into the air. As quickly as the lights dispersed, they reunited and formed the body of the man.

Keix was bewildered. But she heeded her instincts. Drawing on the power that had formed within her, she directed a burst of it into her fist and hit the man again. This time, at the contact, the guy broke apart into smaller bits of lights that flickered for a moment before fading. But her fight was far from over. A dozen other apparitions wearing white jumpsuits, some pristine, some muddied, took the place of the fallen spectre immediately.

Keix panicked. She was employing the same strategy to fight the rest of them, but she could feel her well of power running out. She tried to figure out how to ration the energy as she drew different amounts of it with each blow. Gathering the remaining trace of the power, she hit the last apparition standing before her.

The sparkles dimmed and Keix found herself face to face with Seyfer's soldiers. They were lined up in a tight semicircle, guns directed at her.

Seyfer stood in the middle of the arc, his glowing eyes intrigued. He held up a hand and his troop lowered their weapons.

'You are free to go,' Seyfer said, a slight tremor creeping into his voice.

'What?' Keix thought she was hearing things.

The trooper to Seyfer's right echoed Keix, earning him a withering glare from his commander.

'You have passed the test. You are free to go,' Seyfer waved her away dismissively.

The reprimanded soldier beside him looked down.

Keix couldn't tell if he was submitting to Seyfer or hiding his anger. She was exhausted and filled with questions, but she didn't have to be asked a third time. If Seyfer was letting her go right now, she would go. As she turned on her heel, two thoughts crossed her mind: So much for the fight-to-the-death promise she had made to herself; also, *what the bloody hell just happened?*

7

Request

Keix navigated through the trees without a sound. She kept looking around for signs that she was being tailed because she didn't trust Seyfer. The cool forest air offered little resistance against her speed, and she focused on trying to make sense of her new . . . abilities?

Shot by shot, she analysed what she had felt and seen right after the light rushed at her.

No, not light, she corrected herself. Ghosts—ghosts that the Atros soldiers had released. Or controlled.

She shuddered.

Oron had been right about that. The test that Atros had put them through in their graduation year was nothing compared to the real thing.

Keix remembered the day she had undergone the test. There had been a palpable sense of apprehension among the recruits, but she and Vin had thought nothing of it. Even when the first trooper had emerged from the exam hall looking like he had been drained of half the blood in his body, they had continued to snigger in a corner.

When it was her turn, Keix had stepped into an old classroom repurposed to serve as the exam hall. The stark space held only a bed with straps and a desk. Three monitors and a bundle of colourful wires were atop it. To complete the hostile effect of the set-up, three examiners wearing surgical masks and long white coats stood in the middle of the room, their expressions solemn.

They had strapped Keix onto the bed and nodded at each other. The pain she had experienced was beyond belief. It was like every pore on her skin was being stabbed by a needle, forcefully and repeatedly. Her body had burned from the inside out as she fought to breathe into lungs that felt like they had been liquefied. At the end of it, she had barely been able to stand up. When she had left the room, she had been sure she looked no different from the trooper she had laughed at. Some of the recruits who had fainted from the pain did not graduate. No one spoke of the test after the fact—not even her best friend—all of them preferring to relegate the memory to their subconscious mind.

That test was just a fraction of the torture she had undergone at Atros, but even that couldn't compare with an actual ghost's touch. Not only was the agony a thousand times more intense with the onslaught of the spectre's memories and feelings . . . Keix never wanted to feel that ever again, she thought with a shudder.

'No . . . No . . .' the man's voice had trailed.

Keix could hear him even now, flitting through the woods, carried to her by a gentle wind. The voice sounded like Zej's. She started. Wait a second . . . this wasn't an echo of a memory! She strained her ears. Stomach plummeting, she raced towards the sound, her heart pounding with each step. It crossed her mind that this could well be another trap, but she had to make sure that Zej wasn't in trouble.

Panic shot through her when she reached the source of the disturbance.

Zej's hoverboard lay a few feet away from his unconscious body. His right foot was jutting out at an awkward angle. A section of his hair and half his face was covered with blood pouring from an ugly gash on his forehead.

Three ghosts that had obtained semi-human form surrounded Zej, harnessing his life energy.

Zej's brows drew tight and he continued to murmur a denial. While one of the spirits, a man in a tattered suit, looked heavenward in a show of bliss, another moved in closer to Zej. Keix couldn't tell if this other apparition was male or female. Its skin and features were melted together in a congealed mass.

Keix jumped into action when Zej let out a sharp scream of anguish. The glow in her head that had manifested previously was gone. She tried to make it appear by going through several emotions—coaxing her body into feeling anger, fear, and even happiness, but to no avail. Driven to desperation when Zej gave another tormented shout, Keix reached for the shoulder of one of the phantoms. In an instant, she felt intense pain rip through her. The next moment, however, the power was back and growing.

With a few well-aimed hits, Keix dispatched the spirits. She counted herself lucky that this ragtag trio seemed less aggressive and organized than the ones she had earlier encountered. They had been so engrossed in their 'feeding' that they hadn't even noticed another ready source of life energy nearby.

Rushing to Zej's side, Keix propped his head up onto her bent knee. 'Zej, can you hear me? Zej!'

She looked around; if any enemy was out looking for them, Zej's screams would have alerted them to their location. She needed to get them both out of here as soon as possible. She eased Zej's backpack off and rummaged in it, hoping to find one of his magic plasters for his head wound. But she was straight out of luck. She had to resort to ripping off the bottom of her T-shirt to try to stem the bleeding by binding it tightly against his wound. Blood seeped through the makeshift bandage in record time, darkening it against his pale face and clammy skin.

'Keix?' Zej's voice was soft and raw. His eyelids fluttered. Sweat beaded on his upper lips. 'Need to . . . get out.'

'Where are we exactly?' Keix asked. If only she could get an idea of which sector she was in, she could find a place for them to hide in.

'Danger . . . You.'

'Which sector are we in?' she pressed.

His eyes slid shut and she shook him gently again, barely rousing him. She repeated her question.

'Outside Sector L. North-west.'

Keix deliberated for a moment. Sector L was the outermost section of Atros territory. She had never gone beyond it, except for the last time she had been assigned there. But she knew the sector well enough from studying the maps. The area was flanked by mountain ranges with never-melting ice caps on its right and an endless expanse of woods for the rest of its boundaries. The Atros outpost, a two-storey building with symmetrical, tower-like stone structures at each end, stood at the easternmost edge of the Sector L boundaries. There was no fencing outlining the sector, which meant that Keix could probably sneak into the sector unnoticed. Also, with its next-to-negligible population and numerous abandoned buildings, it might prove easier for them to find a place to hide even if they were risking capture by heading back to Atros territory.

Just as she had made up her mind, Keix heard a scuttling noise in the distance.

'Hey, come on, Zej,' she whispered hurriedly in his ear. 'Let's go.'

The trees around them appeared more spaced out, and the ground was even—a likely indication that there was more frequent foot traffic in this area. They shouldn't be far from the sector.

Keix was surprised when Zej uttered a reply 'Run . . . Leave me . . .'

She had thought he was out cold. She looked at him. Well, he might not be fully unconscious, but there was no way he would be up and running, even without his busted ankle.

Piggyback it is, then, she thought.

As Keix had predicted, there was little difficulty in finding an abandoned building in Sector L, much less one located far from the Atros outpost. Living close to the presence of soldiers provided a sense of comfort for most people, which meant more abandoned buildings further away.

Security within the sector was as lax as she remembered, which was surprising because of the challenge she had faced in getting into the area. Atros troopers dotted the edge of the woods in groups of six, rather than the usual three. They had also upped the frequency of their patrols. Still, the limited visibility during the night allowed Keix to get past them with an unconscious Zej in tow.

Standing by the side of the window in a deserted room, Keix snuck a peek at the streets. A warm flush from the rising sun was creeping across the tarmac pathways, highlighting the cracks and weeds running haphazardly across them, like a budding painter's tentative brushstrokes.

A hunched elderly man with a creaking pushcart filled with cardboard boxes went past the building. He was followed by a young kid in grimy clothes who scuttled across the narrow street. Distant sounds of the sector awakening to a new day drifted in, together with faint smells of exhaust fumes, cheap soap and sewage.

But the scent of freshly baked bread soon overpowered the unpleasant odours, causing Keix's stomach to growl in protest. Her mouth watering, she rubbed her hand over her tummy as if that could mollify the angry sound. She vaguely remembered seeing a sign for a bakery the night before. She thought of popping out to grab some food, but she didn't want to leave Zej alone.

The room they were hiding in was empty except for an old desk that she had moved to barricade the door. She didn't think that anyone was on their tail, but the flimsy piece of furniture would hold up any invaders long enough for them to escape through the single window.

Zej lay on the dusty floor with his backpack and jacket propping up his head. After Keix had brought him here, she had pushed his dislocated ankle back into place, his jacket sleeve stuffed in his mouth; unconscious people could still shout, apparently.

She also rinsed out the cut on his forehead with the water in a bottle she had found in his backpack and rebandaged it with another strip of her T-shirt. She was glad to note that a slight flush was returning to his cheeks and that the bleeding had stemmed, but the wound had swollen into an angry purple bump. It was no wonder he had been out for so long.

Looking at Zej's eyes darting beneath his eyelids, Keix realized she was seeing him in a different light. This was not the same Zej she had known, the one who had grown up with her. The three years that had passed—one spent working with him professionally for Atros and two spent in oblivion—seemed to have matured him beyond his years. There was a hard set to his squarish jaws, now overrun by stubble. Even asleep, his brow was furrowed and his shoulders braced as if they were carrying an invisible weight.

Keix wasn't aware that she had reached out her hand until Zej muttered something in his sleep, stirring. She snatched it back. Did she think that a simple touch could bridge the gulf that yawned between them? The trust and respect that had shattered when he told her of his betrayal of Atros and her—could it be regained?

Zej's eyes shot open and he tried to sit upright, interrupting Keix's contemplations. Blood drained from his face from the exertion.

'Lie down,' she whispered when Zej groaned.

'Man . . . this is a million times worse than the worst hangover I ever had,' Zej said in a hushed and conspiratorial tone.

Keix pursed her lips. Leave it to Zej to figure that humour could diffuse pain. For a split second, she was transported back to the first time they had got drunk together.

'Alright, wrong comparison. It's ten times worse than the time you kicked my ass during our supposed training in Atros,' Zej corrected himself. At her questioning look, he elaborated, 'when you discovered I'd sneak out to a party without you, remember?'

'We weren't training,' Keix corrected him. Zej's memories were not as much memories as they were his version of their shared history. It was a habit he had acquired from hanging around Pod too much. 'I was punished for pulling a prank, made to clean up after the party you "forgot" to tell me about, and you came to piss me off.'

'Right,' Zej pretended to concede. 'I'll pretend I was target practice if you tell me why we are whispering.'

Keix frowned. The head wound *was* bad. 'Don't you remember what happened?'

'Yeah, I got a last-minute invite to an underground party without you and—'

Keix held out a hand to stop him. 'I mean just now. Before this, now.' She gestured to their surroundings.

'Urm,' Zej said with a frown and pause 'I was at the Twin Lounges, doing server maintenance. Then . . .' His expression turned dead serious in an instant, and he snapped his head around, wincing while taking in the scene before him. 'Where's Rold? He sent out a distress signal, and I came as soon as I could. He didn't—' he broke off when he saw Keix's face.

'I'm sorry, Zej. A group of Atros troopers found the safehouse,' Keix explained in a sombre tone. 'Rold pulled the Ifarl card and compelled me to hide in the basement while he faced them. One of them shot him and he had a seizure . . . he was convulsing, white foam spilling out of his mouth. I . . . I couldn't help him.'

Zej's eyes darkened and he brought one of his clenched fists to his bruise and rubbed it, as if the pain helped him to concentrate. It was long moments before he turned to Keix. 'The bullet must have held a cartridge of a sedative developed a couple of years back. It's extremely strong and can sometimes cause violent allergic reactions in those who have Ifarl blood.'

'How do you know that? Wait, are you saying that they didn't mean to kill Rold? They only wanted to capture him?'

Zej shook his head gingerly. 'No. I know what you're thinking, Keix. But only a high-enough dose could cause Rold to have a seizure as violent as the one you described. Even if he doesn't have Ifarl blood, a direct shot would put him into a coma forever. He's—' Zej drew a shuddering breath.

Denial hung thick in the silence that fell between them. Neither wanted to be the first to say the dreaded word out loud. When Keix remained silent, Zej continued, 'The drug—it's what they injected you with during your time in the SOUP. In small doses, it keeps a person in a deep sleep for a limited duration, so you have to re-administer it regularly.' His voice was low and laced with guilt. 'It wasn't meant to be a weapon! We were just looking for a way to—'

'Hold on, *we*? As in Oka or Atros?'

'Atros. I didn't even know Oka existed then. It was one of my research projects after we graduated. We needed to find a way to prevent the spirit population from increasing; which meant keeping people "alive", even after they died, so that they didn't move on and become—'

'—ghosts.'

Zej nodded and seemed a little surprised at her accepting tone.

For some reason, Keix was relieved to hear Zej say out loud that he had not been a spy for a rebel group until after his graduation. She was more than aware that they had joined ATI to do very different things. She had wanted to be the brawn of the operations and Zej, the brain.

But Keix knew the science well enough. When the portal between the worlds had first opened, the hospitals had been worst struck. The radial reverberation of one person dying and turning into a ghost had then caused machines—life-support machines, especially—to fail, resulting in even more deaths. The electromagnetic pulses had also affected different people in different ways. Those with pacemakers, needless to say, were early casualties. But foetuses and newborns were also susceptible to the waves because they interfered with young hearts somehow, altering their rhythm.

Suffice it to say that society's reaction time hadn't been particularly short. But decades later, even with Atros establishing and manning the sector lines and protocols in place to ensure that ghostly invasions were kept to a minimum, the infant mortality rate had remained high. In the numbers game, the balance continually tilted in favour of the other side.

'But the black hole bullets . . .' Keix pushed forward with the questions that she needed answers to now. 'The ghosts shouldn't return after we dispatch them with those?' She meant to state that as an indisputable fact, but the images of a ball of darkness ready to swallow Vin and her troop and then Vin strung up in PEER flashed through her mind as the words left her mouth.

Zej's eyes were full of pity as they scanned Keix's face in the dim light. 'Do you still believe that?'

Prior to this madness, she had never questioned Atros's teachings. Black hole rounds were rare, but standard issue. Troopers had always been taught, during training, about the dangers of using them. If a person was sucked into the black hole whirlpool, he was as good as dead; the person firing the shot would have become, effectively, a murderer.

But now that she thought of it, Atros seemed to have become more lax in drilling this fact home into the troopers who had enrolled a few batches after her. Was that enough grounds for suspicion?

'I—' Keix's voice cracked despite having just spoken. 'I'm not sure what to believe anymore,' she admitted.

Zej let out the breath he had been holding. 'The name is meant to be misleading. Black hole rounds don't create a portal to actual black holes. What they do is initiate a suction portal to one of Atros's secret facilities. Then they . . .' Zej looked sickened at what he was about to say. 'They carry out experiments on the ghosts, justifying it by claiming they need to learn how to subdue—or destroy— them in large numbers, or perhaps even tame them to serve us. *Domestication of ghosts*, Keix! That's what they wanted. There were even whispers of Atros cultivating their own spirit army!'

Keix's heart thundered. She felt a warmth creep up her neck when she recalled Seyfer's 'test'. *Had they actually succeeded? Am I part of the army or just someone they had to get rid of because I could fight ghosts?*

Zej's eyes, dark and glinting, reflected her disgust. Little did she know how different their reasons were for feeling the same way.

'I was ordered to observe and record the tests carried out on these ghosts. I . . .' he hesitated, weighing his next words, 'they are evil, I get it. And we have to find a way to get rid of them. But they were once people too. Imagine if—Oron! The ghost of Oron, being subjected to imprisonment and experiments like gas chambers, or . . . or a room fitted with electrocution panels! What Atros— what *we*, the scientists were doing . . . it just didn't feel right to me. For all their talk about morality and guarding the people, their methods are *twisted*. And you know how they subsequently used some of those tortures on living people they suspected of being spies.'

'Why didn't you tell me?' the words rushed out of Keix. Everything Zej was saying sounded so . . . logical. Puzzle pieces fitting seamlessly together. Like how Atros used to be to her. And right now, it seemed to her that the organization was contradicting itself at every turn.

'You wouldn't have believed me,' Zej answered without a pause. He tried to sit up a little straighter. The conversation seemed to have invigorated him. Not only did he look less confused, his shoulders had relaxed too.

'So you joined Oka? But how did you learn of them?'

Zej shrugged. 'I guess my reluctance was apparent from the way I carried out my duties, and one day, this guy—Sn—Sniper? Snyder? God, why can't I remember the name? I could never have forgotten it!' Zej tapped the heel of his palm on his forehead forcefully.

Keix grabbed his hand and pulled it away. 'Don't do that! You'll open up your wound.' True enough, a corner of the cut had started oozing blood again. But Zej didn't seem to notice. Instead, he rummaged through his backpack and drew out his tablet.

He made some quick swipes on the device and uttered, 'Seyfer.'

Keix's blood froze in her veins. Goosebumps dotted her arms and she almost jumped back when he turned the tablet to her, revealing the exact same Atros soldier from before—the one who had *let* her go. The only difference was that his eyes in the picture were neither glowing nor yellow; they were the complete opposite, a black so deep it looked like it could swallow the lights around it.

'This guy, Seyfer, he came to ask me if I knew anything about Oka,' Zej continued, oblivious to Keix's horrified reaction. 'Of course I didn't, not at that point in time. And I was surprised when he took me at my word and left. I still can't figure out why.'

He continued, 'Anyway, I did some digging. I managed to speak to a handful of them anonymously. I tracked one of their ground operations for a while and found out about how they were helping the families of people who had "mysteriously" disappeared while working various odd jobs for Atros. I dug deeper. Found more evidence of Atros's cover-ups. It just . . . kind of blew my mind when it turned out that Oka wasn't some fanatic rebel group. So I joined them and remained a spy in Atros.'

Keix scrutinized the photo. The image was a little blurry and it was obvious that it was a poorly taken picture of a hardcopy file. Seyfer's face was skewed, but the words accompanying it were legible.

NAME: SEYFER

AGE: 19

RACE: CLASSIFIED

SKILLS: ALL CLASSES

STATUS: CLASSIFIED

The rest of the text was blacked out. When Keix turned to Zej, she was aware that her distress was written on her face—something she wasn't accustomed to doing.

Zej studied her, confused. Then his voice turned cold. 'Do you know him?'

'I—' Keix started, then she took a deep breath. 'He was the one who shot Rold.'

Zej's lips thinned but he said nothing. If Keix wanted any further confirmation that Zej had changed, the hardened glare he was aiming at his tablet would have done it.

'How did you get this?' Keix asked. Without considering how Zej would react, she swiped the screen of the tablet to see if there was any more incriminating evidence.

There were more profiles but Keix couldn't identify them. Seyfer's crew had not taken their helmets off throughout their confrontation. But as she scanned the photos, she saw words like, 'UNDETERMINED' and 'HUMAN' under the 'RACE' heading, 'FIRST CLASS - HAND COMBAT' and 'THIRD CLASS - FIREARMS' under 'SKILLS', and 'ELECTROCUTION' and 'DEATH BY GHOSTS' under 'STATUS', which made her stomach churn.

When she finally turned back to Zej, he posed a question of his own instead of answering hers. 'Keix,' he began with a little hesitation. 'I know how you feel about Atros. I know you're confused, or that you're resisting confronting the truth, thinking this is one huge conspiracy. Our upbringing, the beliefs embedded in us since we were young—these are not things that can change overnight, no matter how much we will it,' Zej said with a tinge of regret in his voice. 'But look at me. Look at me and tell me that I shouldn't be questioning Atros. Tell me that *I* managed to brainwash Pod into joining Oka. Or tell me that what you've experienced so far, since the attack on Sector L, is not enough for you to turn against Atros.'

Keix clenched her fists. She didn't know what to say.

'I want to say this is your choice,' Zej continued, 'to ask you to *choose* to join us. But the truth is, there is nowhere you can go. Atros is hunting you. We may not be able to promise you absolute safety, but I'm quite certain that's not what you're looking for.' His eyes were filled with passion, suppressed anger and a little pity. He had just laid her exact thoughts out in the open.

But what else could she do? A laughing image of a girl with pink hair came to her mind. 'Vin!' Keix exclaimed, startling Zej. Getting her best friend back was a tangible course of action.

'You want me to join your rebellion? Fine,' she said in a determined voice. 'I saw Vin at PEER. You are going to help me to get her out.'

8

Escape

'What do you mean "No"?' asked Keix. The single word of denial bounced around the abandoned room. Heat crept up the back of her neck and the surrounding air suddenly seemed stuffy and cloying.

'I meant, not now. We can't risk it,' said Zej in a loud whisper, getting to his feet while his eyes darted from the window to the door. 'We got you out and Atros came for you. What makes you think that they haven't stepped up the security at PEER?'

Recalling the increased number of patrols at the sector borders, Keix bit back a retort.

'But we have to do something! *Now*. I *have* to,' she insisted, her voice dropping lower. That she had to resort to asking someone for help, even if that person was Zej, chafed her pride. But the self-doubt gnawed at the back of her mind like an insidious parasite—it not only undermined her ability to infiltrate PEER on a solo mission, it forced her to acknowledge that, for the first time since her mother's death, she was at a loss. She thought she heard her self-righteous snarky self sniggering at her previous faith in her own invincibility.

'What if they're experimenting on her—doing horrible things to her?' she added. She thought about Vin's unkempt condition. 'I *know* they are.'

Zej looked uneasy and indignant at the same time.

Pressing on, Keix said, 'Vin was chained up to the wall when I saw her. At least find out for me what they're doing to her.'

A stony silence met her request. Behind Zej's bright eyes, she saw the complex play of emotions and an unfamiliar calculating look that sent a wave of apprehension down her spine. Just as her patience was running out, Zej spoke.

'I'll try—' he raised a hand to pre-empt Keix's objection. 'But I can't promise you anything beyond that.'

Keix nodded.

Zej's eyes widened a little at her immediate compliance. 'What if your worst suspicions are confirmed?'

'Then we can discuss our next move,' said Keix without hesitation. She had been anticipating this line of questioning.

'Discuss?' A short laugh escaped Zej. 'You mean you'd ask who's with you, grab whatever equipment or weapon's necessary, then try to infiltrate PEER to rescue Vin—even though you know it would be a suicide mission.'

'I didn't say—' Keix began, but a shouted command that cut through the silence spared her the need to defend herself further.

A man's voice came through the window, loud and clear. 'Fall in! I want a thorough grid search of the sector. I don't care if you have to poke your head into the sewage canal. As long as there is a heat signature, you will check it out! We *will* find the fugitive, is that understood?'

To a chorus of agreement from outside, Zej patted down his pockets. 'My walkie—I must have lost it during the struggle. There's no way to contact Maii and Pod.' He moved to the window and snuck a peek through it.

Past Zej's shoulders, Keix saw the troopers lining up in an orderly manner in front of a commander she didn't recognize. The fact that they were right outside the building made her heart plummet. Had they detected two heat signatures in this room already?

Pushing pointless thoughts aside, Keix helped Zej shift the desk she had stuck by the door and both of them moved out into the corridor without a sound. Just as they were about to sneak through the main door of the building, a group of troopers moved into view.

Keix and Zej had barely enough time to run up the stairs by the side of the main entrance. They rushed through the first door they came across, into a room that was barely the size of the tiny closet in her Sector L dormitory. Facing each other, with their backs pressed against the wall, the two of them stood in tense silence.

Keix could feel the warmth of Zej's body in the tiny space. His measured breaths caused her hair to tickle her nose and made her want to sneeze. It was only through sheer willpower that she managed not to.

The room also smelled suspiciously like a dumpster, so Keix turned her acute sense of smell down until the stench was just an afterthought—another perk of her Kulcan descent was being able to control just how much she wanted to smell.

A thin strip of orange light gleamed beneath the door. There was just enough light for Keix to see that she and Zej were standing by a hatch—through which, most likely, the previous occupants of the building threw out their trash.

The pounding of her heart was soon drowned out by the heavy-booted footsteps of the troopers in the corridor outside. She picked up some beeping sounds from beyond the flimsy door and her heart sank when a blanket of foreboding silence fell.

When Zej's hand brushed against her thigh, Keix almost jumped. 'Close your eyes and hold your breath,' he whispered into her ear. She caught sight of a device with a blinking orange dot in his hands and barely had a millisecond to comply before he pushed her flat against the gap behind the door just as it burst open with bang.

Zej's push forced the air out of Keix's lungs, but she kept her eyes squeezed shut. He grunted in pain as the door slammed against his back. A hissing sound filled the air. The blinding flash that followed looked like a snapshot from a raging fire through her eyelids.

Pulling a momentarily stunned Keix out from behind the door, Zej rammed his elbow into the chest of the first trooper he saw and knocked off his helmet before slamming his head against the wall.

The burst of light in Keix's eyes faded just in time for her to see the trooper crumple to the floor. She whirled around and stood back to back with Zej as four more uniformed figures advanced on them.

Executing a well-aimed chop at the nearest trooper's neck, she made him stumble backwards and trip on the first soldier that Zej had dispatched. His arms flailed as he tried to break his fall. But the sleeve of his uniform snagged on a sharp protruding nail on the wall. Keix heard a distinct pop as his shoulder dislocated before he fell to the floor howling in pain.

At his shout of pain, the remaining troopers cast a quick glance at their fallen comrades.

Keix took advantage of their hesitation to pounce on the bigger one, hooking her arm around his neck. She made short work of the fight as the soldier tried to shake her off with weak punches that caught only air. His companion ran off when she relaxed her grip on the limp body.

Zej was having trouble with a petite trooper who was holding on like a leech to his back, her helmet having come off some time during the struggle.

Keix grabbed the girl by her mussed-up braid and yanked her backwards, causing her to loosen her grip on Zej before shoving her towards the nearest wall. There was a dull thud as her skull made contact with the floor.

Zej managed to utter a word of thanks to Keix through his tear-filled eyes.

'One of them just ran off to get backup, I think,' Keix waved him over. 'We should get going.'

Another figure appeared at the top of the stairs as they made their way across the mangled bodies. Keix and Zej tensed for another fight.

'Whoa, whoa! Just wait—wait!' The newcomer held up his hands to signal that he was not a threat. But Keix recognized his voice.

'You!' she gasped, raising a fist towards him.

'Yes, me! I'm here to help.' He pulled off his helmet, revealing a mass of blue curls and brows to match. His high cheekbones and sharp chin gave him a youthful charm, but his intelligent dark eyes made her think that he was probably a few years older than Zej. He frowned. 'Wait a minute . . . What do you mean "you"? You know me?'

Keix ignored his questions. Instead, she scoffed, 'Help!?' Waving at the confusion around her, she continued, 'You're the leader of this group.'

'Oh, yeah,' he said nonplussed as soon as he grasped Keix's meaning. To Zej, he added, 'Anyway, Machillian says your cover's blown. He wants you back straight away.'

'Hold on . . .' said Keix in disbelief. 'You're with Oka too?' She turned to Zej and added, 'Do you know him? How many of you are there exactly?'

Zej seemed to be scrutinizing the trooper, but he shrugged at Keix's questions.

'To answer your questions: Yes. No, and not enough. I'm J—single alphabet—by the way,' he said, bending down to pull the boots off of one of the unconscious troopers. 'You shouldn't have returned to the sectors. Security's been crazy tight since your escape from PEER.'

'You know me?' Keix asked in surprise.

'Yeah, K. You're on the "Most Wanted" list now. Traitor. Spy. Rebel,' said J, ticking off each descriptor with a finger. 'You too, Z,' he said to Zej while unbuttoning his teammate's uniform. 'The two of you are going to need disguises to leave the sector. What are you standing there for? Get cracking!' he added, when he raised his head to see Keix still rooted to the spot.

Keix turned to see Zej doing the same thing as J. In fact, he was already pulling on the uniform. At her questioning look, he shrugged and said, 'He knows Machillian,' as if that settled everything.

Keix was flabbergasted by this logic. *I know you and Pod, so does that mean I'm part of Oka too?* she wanted to ask.

'And you have just one minute and forty-three seconds left before Atros's backup arrives,' J said, checking his watch.

'We have to get moving,' Zej said to Keix. He straightened up and picked up two batons from the bodies on the ground and threw one to Keix who caught it automatically.

Seeing that her choices were seriously limited to either going with Zej or taking down J and running off on her own, she pulled on a uniform and helmet too, wondering if she'd used up all the luck she had left in her life. First Seyfer, now J.

'You know the rendezvous point?' said J.

'Yeah, I do,' replied Zej, nodding to J.

'Good luck. You're going to need it,' said J, bringing two fingers to his temple and flicking them in the direction of Keix.

Turning on her heel, Keix followed Zej down the stairs and out of the building.

'How do you know that you can trust that J?' Keix asked Zej as soon as they were a safe distance from the building.

She kept throwing glances over her shoulder like she was having a twitch.

'I don't,' replied Zej. 'But Machillian's our leader. If J knows his name, it means he's aware of more . . .'

'So we could be walking into a potential trap?' muttered Keix from the corner of her mouth as two Atros soldiers walked past them without a second look.

'We're going to investigate. If J's really with Oka, we'll be the luckiest fugitives in the world. If not . . .' Zej trailed off as he turned into a narrow alley flanked by two tall, abandoned buildings.

Although the sun was now high in the sky bathing the entire sector in light, the alleyway looked dank and gloomy from the shadows cast by the disused structures.

'Where is this rendezvous point, anyway?' asked Keix, keeping pace with Zej. She looked behind them again. There was no sign of the two Atros soldiers from seconds ago. Another thought struck her. 'What if he let us go as bait?'

Zej stopped in his tracks and turned to face her. After a second of silence, he replied, 'It's a risk I'm willing to take.'

Before Keix could contemplate the meaning behind his words, Zej had bent down and pulled up a manhole cover.

Keix pulled off her helmet and stared at him.

'It's the fastest way out of the sector,' said Zej.

'But J just told his unit to search for us in the sewage canal if they had to,' said Keix, incredulous.

Zej's laughter was muffled by his helmet. 'He was joking. Probably. And it's not a sewage pipe.'

At Keix's raised eyebrow, Zej laughed again.

'Well, not entirely. Anyway, it's hard to locate a proper heat signature through these underground pipes. Plus, Atros is going to need more than invisibility suits to be able to tail us in there.' He sat down and swung both his legs into the hole. 'You'll see.'

Keix saw what Zej meant once she set foot in the tunnel and looked around.

Inches-deep sludge covered the curved floor of the pipes and squishing sounds followed every step that they took. Tracking lights that ran along the length of the pipes cast dancing shadows everywhere. The pipes also didn't seem to have any sort of discernible pattern, forking and rounding off at irregular intervals—it seemed near impossible to navigate these tunnels, much less follow someone without drawing their attention.

The only downside of this escape plan was the putrid smell permeating the cool surrounding air. If Keix was gagging even with her sense of smell turned all the way down, she didn't want to imagine how Zej was breathing the air without any visible discomfort.

Yet in spite of his head injury, Zej led Keix through each turn and around each corner with purposeful strides, barely stopping to rest, as if he actually had a clear idea of where they were supposed to be headed. When doubts swarmed within her, she kept reminding herself that she was only along for the ride because of his recent concussion. But that didn't stop her from glaring at his back when he picked up his pace and insisted that they were on the right track. If he could manage, despite his ankle injury, she sure as hell wasn't going to complain about the less-than-ideal conditions they were in.

A shower—long and hot, if possible. Rest. Food. Information. That's all I need, she reassured herself. *Then I'll sneak off and make my own plans to save Vin. I won't get involved with Oka, no matter what Zej and Pod say*, Keix promised herself.

When they finally surfaced, Keix estimated that they must have spent no less than fourteen hours in the pipes judging by the position of the moon. She was surprised to see that the exit that they had taken led to the fringes of a lush, sprawling forest. From the lack of activity, bright lights and fences, she figured they must be a fair distance away from the nearest sector.

'*This* is the meeting point?' asked Keix.

'No, *that* is,' replied Zej, pointing to a spot on the horizon. 'It should take about three hours for us to get there on foot.'

Outlined against the bluish grey night sky were several tall, cone-shaped buildings dispersed between shorter rectangular ones. Taking a straight route there seemed plausible since the landscape that stretched out before them looked flat and there were no signs of any huge obstacles.

The walk to the meeting point proved as uneventful as the sewage pipe excursion. The trees provided just enough cover and the distance from the sector boundaries meant chances of running into Atros soldiers were slim. Between the dimly lit, snaking tunnels and the fresh air and open space, Keix thought their current situation was a major upgrade. They even managed to stop by a rushing stream along the way to wash some of the gunk off their faces and arms. By the soft glow of the crescent moon, she could still see the angry bump on Zej's head. The cut wasn't bleeding anymore, but after being covered in waste for hours, infection seemed imminent.

They made it to the building in record time, with half an hour to spare. Up close, Keix was surprised that it wasn't another abandoned building, although the exterior paint job looked like it had seen better days. The air was suffused with the smell of disinfectant mixed with the woody scent of the forest nearby. Besides the gentle rustling of a breeze, her sharp hearing could only pick up a faint hum coming from nowhere in particular. A third of the overhead lights were in operation and the security post was manned by a guard who was clearly dozing off. The sign next to the main gate said that this was a sewage and recycling plant outside Sector M.

Keix reviewed their position. Sector M was an outlying sector, like Sector L. They shared a neighbour, Sector H, with L on its left and M on its right. Both Sectors H and M were much livelier neighbourhoods compared to the deserted Sector L.

Zej led her away from the guard and around the back of the facility where he picked a lock along the fence and ushered her in.

'Looks like we're in luck,' whispered Zej.

At Keix's sceptical look, he explained, 'Atros has been planning to shut this plant down soon so it is minimally manned. We have a guy on the inside who knows the out-of-bounds areas, so we sometimes hold meetings here. It's near enough to the city centre for us to drop by without arousing suspicion. And it doesn't look like we're getting ambushed anytime soon.'

'How do you know they're not already inside, waiting to get the jump on us?' asked Keix.

Zej shrugged. 'The canals are the fastest way here. And there's no way anyone could have followed us through the pipes without us noticing. If Atros had found our trail or dispatched soldiers to stalk us, we would have seen telltale signs of that on the way here because of the lack of cover.' He led Keix through one of the narrower pathways in the plant to a heavy, unmarked steel door. Just as he was reaching for the handle, the door swung open, away from him.

'Hurry in,' a rich, male voice drawled.

Keix tensed. The speaker was concealed by the door and the pitch-black doorway that yawned beyond, rendering him almost invisible.

Sensing her hesitation, Zej put his hand on the small of her back to urge her forward. Despite that, his voice was tight when he whispered in her ear. 'Don't worry. I know him.'

'Yeah, Zej and I go *way* back. Name's Dace. You must be Keix,' the new guy said as he closed the door behind them. Once it was secured, the lights within the building came on, revealing a length of spiral steel steps going both upward and down.

Dace gestured towards the steps going down. 'We go down four floors.'

Zej went first. Making her way down the steps, sandwiched between him and Dace, Keix couldn't help but try to fish for some information. 'How did you know we were coming?'

'J sent word. I've been waiting and watching in the control room after that,' Dace replied in a matter-of-fact way.

'Are you the only one here?'

'Yeah. I would have gone out to get you but since I'm the only one on duty, got to stay by the control room to await *orders*. Right, Zej?'

Zej stiffened but gave no reply.

Keix's eyes swivelled between them. She wondered what might be up with these two, but decided that figuring out their drama was the lowest of her priorities right now.

'We're here,' Zej interrupted the awkward silence, pushing open another heavy steel door.

'Please. No sitting until you get yourselves cleaned up.' Dace skittered past Keix and Zej, taking great care to avoid contact with them.

The room they had stepped into was spacious, with yellowed paint peeling in random spots. A plush three-seater sofa sat against the wall opposite the door they had entered through. To the left of the sofa was a nondescript arch that led to a corridor, and in front of the sofa was a wooden coffee table with a stack of frozen pizza packaging and some crushed beer cans. A series of screens from the ceiling to a waist-high table paired with a cushy office chair was arranged against the other side of the wall. The eclectic mix of furniture was pretty cosy, yet somewhat bizarre at the same time.

Under the well-lit conditions, Keix saw that Dace was about a head taller than Zej. Even wearing a ratty T-shirt, khaki shorts and lounge slippers, Keix couldn't help but steal another look at his well-built physique. Long, messy ginger curls completed his look, but within the depths of his light teal-coloured eyes, she detected a trace of sadness that was completely at odds with his cocky bearing.

The tension between Dace and Zej was palpable. Dace was staring straight at Zej with an outwardly hostile attitude, while Zej was looking anywhere but at his colleague.

Before Keix could form a coherent question for either of them, Zej hurried down the hallway, muttering something about getting cleaned up.

'Here,' Dace's voice cut through Keix's confusion. 'I'll show you where you go to get cleaned up. We'll talk more after we make sure you're not fouling up my digs further.'

'What's going on with you two?' Keix gestured to the corridor. Zej was nowhere to be seen.

Dace shrugged. 'What's going on with *you two*?'

'Huh?' Keix had no idea where this conversation was going.

At the look on her face, Dace gave a hoot of laughter and gestured for her to follow him through the same hallway that Zej had disappeared into. It was long and connected to other corridors, and it reminded Keix of the underground pipes from before—except this time, instead of Zej, Dace was the one taking the lead.

They stopped by one of the utility rooms to grab a fresh change of clothes and towel before he brought her to an empty bathroom, rectangular and tiled in a white and grey hexagonal mosaic. Showerheads and basins were spaced out along opposite lengths of walls, and there was a knee-high fluorescent light placed near the entrance.

Dace pointed to some toiletries, and a portable gas stove and kettle on the basin countertop. 'Figured you'd want a hot shower. But you'll have to boil your own water. That's the best I can do on such short notice. This part of the plant's supposedly shut down, so we're only drawing enough power for the "necessities" like lights and control panel to avoid suspicion—or so *orders* say.'

Taken aback by his thoughtfulness, Keix nodded gratefully. 'That's good enough. Thanks.'

'Well, too bad that's not good enough for me. I mean just saying thanks. You have to take me out to dinner. As long as it's not reheated pizza,' he gave an exaggerated shudder, 'I'll bite. And it has to be far away from here. Not that guarding an abandoned sewage plant isn't great fun, but sometimes it stinks—literally, and other times, figuratively. You know?'

Keix laughed. Perhaps it was Dace's roguish charm or his good looks, or the fact that he reminded her of Pod, she couldn't help but feel at ease with him. 'Do you have news of Pod?' she asked, worry evident in her voice. 'Or Maii?'

Dace shook his head solemnly. 'There's a briefing tomorrow afternoon. We should know more then. By the way, you can latch the door from the inside.' He pointed to the entrance. 'I'll fill you in on what I know after you're done here.'

Keix nodded again. 'Thanks, Dace.' She saw him smile as he turned to leave.

Raising his right hand to his side, he shook two fingers at Keix. 'That's two dinners, then.'

Left to her own devices, Keix's thoughts swirled. She hoped she was not too late to save Vin. Come to think of it, if Vin was stuck in PEER, the rest of the soldiers who had responded to the paranormal attack at Sector L, including Lyndon, could very well be there too.

And not to mention the mysterious well of power that she had discovered when she was facing down Seyfer's ghosts. She tried to do the same now, reaching within herself, but . . .

Nothing. Her frustration grew. Too many questions, too few answers.

'Damn it!' Keix muttered, banging her fist on the countertop and glaring at her reflection in the aged mirror. By the stark light cast by the lamp, the dark circles around her eyes and her cheekbones appeared more pronounced than ever. Sections of her recently cut hair were matted and stuck out at odd angles, making her look like a cartoonish depiction of someone who had just undergone electrocution. The face in the mirror twisted into a wry smile. *Close enough*, she thought.

9

The Key

Six kettles of boiled water and almost an entire bottle each of shampoo and shower gel later, Keix emerged from the shower in a slightly better mood. She almost jumped when she found Dace leaning against the corridor, making rhythmic clinks as he stirred a cup.

He gave a low whistle when he saw her. 'You clean up well,' he said, pretending to sniff the air. 'And you smell sweet. Too sweet, I think. Well, maybe I'll develop a liking for it, who knows?'

Keix stared at him before narrowing her eyes. 'Wait. How did you know I was done? Were there cameras in there?' she waved to the bathroom.

'Oh, how you wound me, Keix. I am many things, but an opportunistic voyeur I am not.' Dace sounded outraged, but the gleam in his eyes told Keix that he was not the least offended. 'I've been waiting here for,' he checked his watch, 'the past twenty-two minutes. Look, even the instant soup I made for you has cooled.' He held out the cup.

Keix's stomach growled at the savoury smell.

'Here,' Dace said, passing the cup to Keix and turning to go back down the hallway. 'I'm heating up some frozen pizza too. Bet you'll be a heartbreaker like me once you pack some muscles on that scrawny frame of yours.'

Tagging along behind him, Keix sipped at the soup Dace had prepared. Even though it was lukewarm, her tummy welcomed any source of food it could get. 'Where's Zej? How is he?'

'Oh, Zej's fine. He's probably resting,' Dace gave a dismissive wave, 'somewhere.'

'What's your problem with him?'

Dace feigned astonishment. 'And here I was, thinking that I'm a master at hiding my hostile feelings. How'd you figure that out?'

'How, indeed,' Keix paused, pretending to give his question deep thought. 'Probably from the dripping sarcasm in your voice when you mention him?' They were approaching the control room and the smell of pizza made Keix's mouth water.

Dace chortled. '*I like you*, Keix. So glad you're here so I don't have to face Killjoy Kaplan alone. Ah, there he is.' He pointed in the direction of the control panel where a hunched figure was sitting. Reaching past the corner of Kaplan's seat, Dace retrieved a small torchlight and a package similar to the frozen pizza ones Keix had seen on the coffee table. 'Kaplan, Keix. Keix, Kaplan.'

Kaplan turned out to be a guy in his thirties who reminded Keix of an Odat. His eyes, framed by thick goggle-like glasses, were widely spaced above a flat nose on his broad face. In his starched shirt, black-grey pinstriped pants and polished boots, he looked no different from a disgruntled office worker. Paper-thin lips set in a permanently sour expression reinforced the glum image.

Keix figured that it was with great reluctance that Kaplan tore his eyes away from the screens because, after a cursory glance and nod in her direction, he immediately whipped his head back to stare intently at the control panels again.

Dace gave Keix a shrug at Kaplan's lack of manners and steered her back in the direction of the showers. 'His lack of enthusiasm for anything not related to staring at the screens drives me nuts. Every time I talk to him, he gives me that signature blank look of his. I swear, that's his one and only expression. Except when he comes for his shift, then he gives me this grunt, which is one of the most coherent sounds he can put together, by way of greeting.'

Keix smiled at Dace's assessment of Kaplan. She didn't want to judge, but Kaplan did seem like a bore. 'At least he pays attention to security.'

'Tsk, tsk. Sometimes you miss out the details when you've been staring at something for too long. Honestly, it's a wonder he sees anything through those goggles.'

Instead of fuelling Dace's bias against Kaplan, Keix changed the topic. 'Where are we going?' she asked. They were now following the beam of the torch, going down an unmarked winding route long past the showers and up several flights of stairs.

'Away from prying eyes and ears. And to where the air's fresher. As fresh as it gets around here, anyway.' Dace stopped in front of a wooden door and pushed it open. Stepping into the room, he held the door open for Keix and closed it soundlessly behind her.

Moonlight was streaming into the squarish room through glass windows. One of them was slightly ajar, and the gentle wind gave a low whistle as it entered the abandoned space through the slit. Desks and chairs were strewn around in a haphazard manner and from the shabby writing board, Keix assumed it was an old classroom of sorts.

Dace pulled up a dusty table and set the pizza package on it. Dragging up two chairs, he made a show of brushing the dirt off one of them and presenting it to Keix with a bow.

'Are you always this flippant?' Keix asked, accepting the gesture with an incline of her head.

'I am always *chivalrous* to beautiful women—especially one I cannot beat in a fist-to-fist fight,' Dace said, taking his seat opposite her. At Keix's questioning look, he continued, 'I made it a point to find out what I could about you when Oka made you into a priority rescue case. Anyway, I'm sure you have a ton of things to ask me. Shoot.'

Keix hesitated. Should she be suspicious that Dace was being—or pretending to be—so forthcoming? After all, while she had known Zej or Pod for years, she had only met Dace less than two hours ago. 'Don't you have orders that prevent you from divulging sensitive information to me?' she asked, narrowing her eyes.

'*Orders* . . . are not so much orders to me as they are guidelines,' he said with bitterness. 'Let me put it this way: If an order requires you to sacrifice your life to save thousands of others—would you do it?'

Keix stuffed a slice of pizza into her mouth so she would be spared the need to answer. Atros soldiers always put the safety of the sectors and citizens before themselves. It was what made them the best people to defend the city against threats, supernatural or otherwise. But that was before Sector L, before PEER and the new perspective she had gained since then.

'Better yet, what if the order requires you to sacrifice someone else's life to save millions of others?' Dace asked, with a touch more agitation.

Thinking back to the night when Vin's troop had been attacked by ghosts, a sense of guilt crept into Keix's heart. That was exactly what she had done—sacrificed a few lives for the greater good. The question she never thought she would ask herself was, *was it truly a small sacrifice?* 'I—'

'But,' Dace interrupted, his mien lightening in an instant, 'now's not the time for philosophical discussions. Sorry I waylaid you.'

Keix pushed the disturbing seed of doubt that Dace had planted in her head away with much difficulty and a torrent of questions spilled from her. 'Where are we? What does Oka want with me? What's their beef with Atros?'

To her mild surprise, she found out that Dace was capable of holding a conversation without levity or venturing onto too-solemn grounds. Still, there was not much he said that she hadn't figured out for herself; Oka, like Atros, seemed to be big on secrets. *Like every other race and organization that I can think of,* she thought.

He placed the sewage plant at an hours' drive from the Sector M borders and half a day's drive from the city centre. Sector M was much bigger in size compared to the sectors near the city centre, but it was only about half the size of Sector L. The sewage plant had been built to service Sector M, but in the past two years, people had started moving nearer to the city centre for better security and better job opportunities. Eventually, the drop in population made it no longer sensible to keep the facility running, so they were in the midst of closing it down.

What shocked Keix was when Dace mentioned his theory that this place was a neutral ground for the Ifarls that Oka kept in contact with. Rold had told her just the opposite—that these two groups were not related in the least.

'As far as I know, all the meetings Oka have with Ifarls have taken place here. And I'm not talking about your garden-variety Ifarls. From their ages and the way they behave, they'd have to be elders—or elder-trainees, or whatever you call those elder material ones, for sure,' Dace concluded. 'Of course, small fry like me have never been invited into these meetings—though it isn't for lack of trying,' he added with a cheeky smile.

Keix wondered if Dace was telling the truth. If so, what kind of business could Ifarl elders have with Oka? Even 'garden-variety' Ifarls were notoriously mysterious, not to mention their almighty elders. 'And where do I fit in? If I even do?' she asked.

Dace shrugged. 'All I know is Zej pulled some serious strings to launch a rescue mission for you. He must have had a super-convincing argument too. I've never heard of, or seen, Oka doing infiltration and rescue—the risk of exposing any spy of theirs, highly placed or not, does serious damage to their operations. Take Zej, for example. He's now on Atros's Wanted List. Like you. He'll be hard to replace. We all know that the research department holds the most tantalizing secrets.'

Dace continued to fill Keix in on certain operations and spy work that Oka engaged in. Summing it up, she thought that Oka were more focused on gathering intel than doing anything useful with it. But they did send out their people to help villages and communities that didn't want anything to do with Atros and those who had a beef with Atros, like Zej had told her before—which actually sounded quite decent to her.

'Do you know where I can get supplies like invisibility suits or weapons?' asked Keix, trying to tick off the list of things that she thought she needed to get Vin out of PEER. She wasn't confident she would be able to pull it off on her own; in fact, the reason why she wasn't barging into the facility right now was because she was hoping to convince at least Pod and Zej to join her somehow.

'It's a suicide mission, you know,' said Dace with a meaningful look.

Keix opened her mouth to protest but he cut her off.

'I'll see if I can get us a couple.'

'Us? No . . . I'm not bringing you with me.'

'Why not?'

'You just said it yourself. It's a suicide mission. Why would you risk your life for someone you don't know? Wait a minute . . . you don't know Vin, do you?'

'You're going to rescue a person called Vin?'

Keix was flabbergasted. 'What did you think I was going to do?'

'Something rebellious, of course. And likely, dangerous,' he said with a smirk.

'And you were volunteering without knowing what it was?'

Dace shrugged and looked out of the window. He seemed mesmerized by the soft orange glow spreading like watercolour paint across the indigo sky from the horizon.

The sight reminded Keix of Rold and it felt like someone had plunged her heart into a bucket of ice.

Instead of pressing the issue, Keix asked, 'Do you know of an Acquisitions team or department in Atros?'

'Acquisitions?' Dace repeated with a frown. He seemed unfazed by the sudden change of topic but pondered for a long while before answering, 'No. I've never heard of it in my life.'

Another dead-end, Keix thought, frustrated. Then another idea struck her. *Since I'm running headlong into impasses, might as well try another.* 'Do you have a phone I can borrow?' she asked a thoughtful Dace, who seemed surprised.

But he reached into his trouser pocket and produced a slim rectangular mobile without hesitation. 'Are you giving me your number? I'll last a couple of hours, at the most, before I start texting you,' he joked.

That earned a laugh from Keix. 'Is the line secure?' she asked.

'Encrypted with higher-than-Oka-level technology,' he confirmed. 'Wouldn't want anyone to find out about our speed-of-light scandalous romance, would we?'

Keix laughed again when he winked. Her heart was pounding but her excitement had nothing to do with Dace's flirting. Taking a deep breath, she keyed in Oron's number and tapped the connect button. The milliseconds seemed to stretch out as she held her breath in anticipation. As soon as she heard a mechanized voice, her heart fell. Invalid number.

Sighing, Keix tried her voicemail number next without conscious thought. Dace waited patiently while she listened to her messages. Half of them were from Pod; the earliest messages were delivered by his joking self, inviting her to some party, asking her to call him back soon before they got increasingly worried and short. The other half of her messages were dominated by static and airy sounds before the person on the other line hung up. When she got to her last message, she almost couldn't believe her ears. The voice on the other end was unmistakably Oron's. He didn't even have to identify himself. His tone was clipped, more so than she remembered, when he said just three short words, 'Trust your friend.'

Keix stirred from a fitful sleep when she felt a warm puff of air in her face. She groaned, squeezing her eyes shut as she buried her head in the pillow. The sudden burst of bright light was threatening to scorch the insides of her eyelids. For a moment, she couldn't recall where she was. Then Oron's voice message replayed in her head, overshadowing the pounding pain within. 'Trust your friend,' he had said. Such a succinct sentence. One that plagued her from the moment she heard it.

Dace had picked up on her reticent mood after the call and perceptively kept himself from making any comments about it as he escorted her back to a bare room near the showers. She had lain on the only piece of furniture in the space, a sterile-looking steel bed with a thin foam mattress, trying to process her thoughts until exhaustion overtook her.

Easy-peasy if you know who your friends are, Keix thought, or friend—was the singular term a mistake on Oron's part?

She thought of Vin and tried not to let the guilt overwhelm her.

Another breath of warm air tickled the nape of her neck, followed by a snort of amusement. At the sound, she sat up immediately, her fist reaching out to the nearest object her eyes could discern—

'Pod?' Keix snatched her hand back, which would have connected with Pod's eye if he had not straightened up. She assumed that he had taken a much more sanitary route than Zej and her from the look of his usual ensemble—this time, a wrinkled red T-shirt read, *My* (then stacked on top of each other) *Best; Girl; Boy; Only;* followed by a bigger *Friend*, under a cartoonish drawing of a game console. Relief flooded her and she launched herself into the arms of a laughing Pod. 'I thought they got you.'

'Well, if they did, I would have missed out on a great opportunity to try and dodge one of your legendary punches, eh? *And* the chance to test one of my irritation skills on you.'

'Which is?' Keix asked suspiciously. She must have been completely worn out if Pod was able to get the jump on her.

'Blowing air into your face while you're sleeping to try and wake you up.'

There were no windows in this room, recalled Keix. 'Urgh! How childish can you get!' She pulled on Pod's sleeve and tried to wipe her face and nape on it.

Pod laughed. 'On a scale of one to ten? Eleven!'

'Oh, yucks, did you watch me sleep?' Keix gave Pod a shove. 'Tell me no, because that's absolutely cree—'

Suddenly, the door flew open and hit Pod on the back of his head. The room was that tiny. Maii barged in, rage blazing in her eyes. Before Keix could react, Maii had her pinioned to the bed, face-down, by twisting both her arms behind her and straddling her.

Keix was shocked at Maii's ability to hold her down. She was the one who usually had an advantage in a physical fight, especially with someone smaller than her. Could Maii be using some kind of spell to enhance her strength?

'*What the hell!*' shouted Keix, but it came out all muffled because her face was pressed against the pillow. She tried to buck Maii off but only succeeded in twisting her head to face the doorway just in time to see Zej rush in.

'Maii, wait—' Zej said.

The Ifarl's usual sing-song voice dropped to a low timbre as she addressed Keix, totally ignoring Zej, 'What happened to Rold?'

'Maii, I told you. Keix was—' Zej started.

Interrupting him, Maii said, 'I know what you told me. I want to hear what *she* says.' To Keix, she commanded, 'What happened to Rold? Do *not* lie to me.'

Keix bristled. The lack of trust between the two of them went both ways. She would probably have done the same if she were in Maii's shoes, but it didn't mean that she was going to obey without putting up a fight—especially since Zej and Pod seemed perfectly happy to remain spectators in this showdown.

Once again, Keix felt the strange magic of the Ifarl command creeping into her brain, except halfway through, it halted as if it had met an invisible wall and disintegrated. One thing was sure—it wasn't her willpower; the foreign tickling in her head had a signature not unlike the one she had reached out to when she fought the ghosts. Did she just consciously resist an Ifarl command with her 'power'—if she could even call it that? Did Maii feel it? Keix tried to crane her head to see Maii's reaction, but the Ifarl maintained a strong hold on her.

The expectant silence in the room held no answers.

Not wanting to let the rest know what was going through her mind—literally—Keix pretended that she was reorganizing her thoughts. Maii didn't compel her to stop struggling, so that was what she did while she recounted the incident, from when Rold spelled her to hide, to finding an unconscious Zej. She was itching to test the grounds by telling an outright lie, but she didn't want to raise suspicions by saying something different from Zej. So she kept it brief and hedged to keep from everyone how Seyfer let her go and her ability to fight ghosts.

Towards the end of her narrative, Keix felt Maii sag a fraction—from resignation or fatigue, she didn't bother to find out. In the blink of an eye, she used all her strength to tilt her body to the side, throwing Maii off balance and pouncing on top of her.

A crack sounded when Maii's head hit the floor, followed by sharp intakes of breath and whoas from Pod and Zej.

Those irksome boys, Keix thought to herself. I'll deal with them later.

But now, Keix wanted to make a point. With their positions reversed, she bent down to Maii's ear. In a deadly tone, she whispered, 'Do. *Not*. Mess with me. Again.'

Everyone jumped when they heard Dace's voice. He must have snuck in unseen during Keix's retaliation, 'Whoa . . . I hate to break up this steamy scene,' he said, cutting through the tension in the room in a jovial voice, 'but there's something you guys should see. Er, or hear, rather.'

As Dace led them out of the room and down the corridor, he kept shushing them, looking particularly gleeful. Sceptical, but intrigued, Keix and Pod followed close behind him, while Maii, still shooting sparks at Keix's back paced beside a disapproving Zej. Minutes later, the five of them were cramped into a room similar to the one they had vacated several corridors down.

'Okay, so remember when I told you last night that they were having a briefing today?' Dace said to Keix in a whisper. 'Turns out it's a high level one. *Two* Ifarl elders just came in.' To emphasize his point, Dace held out two slender fingers.

'All right . . . so?' Keix asked, matching his low voice.

'So . . . aren't you interested in what they are discussing?' Dace held out a boxy device. He had a wild gleam in his eyes.

Zej reacted before anyone else could. Making no effort to mask his disapproval, he asked in a tight and rather loud voice, 'You're *eavesdropping* on meetings?'

'Shh! They're just three doors down,' Dace said in a slightly louder, but still muted tone. He gave a shrug, but the challenge was apparent when he continued, 'You could turn me in. Go on.'

Keix made a split-second decision. She placed a hand on Zej's arm. 'Wait. Did you know that Oka were meeting with Ifarl elders?'

Peeling his eyes away from Dace, Zej turned to Keix. His closed expression told her that he wasn't privy to that fact, but it was obvious that he was uncomfortable with spying on his superiors, which—Keix refrained from pointing out—was ironic, really.

'I just want to know if they have any information regarding PEER.' Keix mouthed the next words to Zej, her eyes pleading, 'Or Vin.'

Zej held her gaze with a frown, then he cast a questioning glance at Maii, whose look of irritation had been replaced with one of mild interest. Pod's eyes were rounded and his vigorous nodding caught everyone's attention.

'You want in on this?' Zej asked unnecessarily.

'Well, erm . . .' Pod's eager look turned sheepish as he tugged Zej to a corner of the room. In a commendable attempt to prevent the rest of them from hearing what he said next—which failed miserably, considering the size of the space they were in—he lowered his voice to a bare whisper, 'You said it yourself that you were surprised that they sanctioned Keix's rescue. Aren't you the least bit curious about what the higher-ups discuss in their meetings? This could be our only chance to find out.'

Silence followed Pod's words, which was severed by Dace's impatient tone. 'We haven't got all day. We may be missing out important bits of the conversation while you ponder your so-called morals. You're either in or out. If it's the latter, you can leave quietly, or turn us in. Decide now.'

Throwing a dirty look at Dace, Zej reached an internal compromise. 'I'll stay. But whatever we hear in this room, stays in this room. Nothing gets out, am I clear? *Nothing*.'

Dace started fiddling with the device, his smirk firmly in place, while the rest of them expressed their assent. 'This is the furthest we can go without losing the signal. Actually, I tried this out for the first time ten minutes ago, before I went to get you guys,' he said by way of explanation.

After some static interference, voices drifted from the transmitter. They couldn't turn the volume too high, so all of them huddled together around the palm-sized device.

' . . . stepped up patrols at the sector borders, especially Sector L, since the asset we recovered from PEER was last seen there,' a mild and controlled voice said. Keix thought it was a female although she couldn't be sure. 'We were lucky that one of our own was there to aid her escape.'

'*Lucky?*' an exceptionally whiny-sounding male sneered. 'I wouldn't exactly call losing one of our most well-placed spies in the Atros research department lucky.'

Were Oka, like Atros, after me because I can fight ghosts with this weird strand of 'power' within me? Keix wondered. She shuddered to think of the types of experiments she would be subject to should they try to uncover the root of this new ability. Shaking the unpleasant images away, she snuck a look at Zej. She couldn't help but feel a little guilty and sorry for him. After all, he had lost his job and his standing within Oka *and* was now wanted by Atros because he had gone to rescue her from PEER.

The whiny man continued his grousing, 'Atros has been keeping tabs on the older, higher-ranking spies. These new recruits are the only way we can find out if we're being fed—'

'Enough, Flincon,' a raspy and commanding voice interjected. 'Do you have anything constructive to add?'

There was an awkward second of silence before Flincon stuttered, 'I—I . . .' Then he seemed to gather himself and spoke more confidently, 'I think it's unwise to assign so many of our men to acquire an asset, whose worth we have no proof of except for *their* word.'

'Four is hardly many, Flincon,' said the mild-mannered one.

A noticeably mellifluous female voice joined in. 'And it's not only *our* word that made you carry out the rescue mission. You made that decision based on intel you gathered. We alerted you to other subjects, but you chose to only rescue Keix.' There was a definite edge of dislike in her tone. This must be one of the Ifarl elders.

'I thought we were in this together? Then why aren't you sending anyone to help, if you're so all-knowing?' Flincon asked with a raised voice. Keix wondered why this petulant child had been invited at all.

'*We,*' a new rumbling voice said evenly, 'are not "in this together". *We* are not obliged to send our people to help in your foolish fights.' This must be the other Ifarl. Keix glanced around the room and saw the dubiousness she felt reflected in everyone else's faces, except Maii who maintained an air of haughtiness as if she agreed with what was said.

The male Ifarl went on contemptuously, '*We* are here as advisors out of goodwill. Atros's experiments are disrupting the balance of the world, and your little organization stands the best chance of stopping them. The key to this aim is Keix . . .'

10

Agenda

Four pairs of eyes swivelled to Keix's face at the Ifarl's words. She tried to swallow the lump forming in her throat as he continued, his voice dripping with disdain, 'So are the others we've named. Keep Atros from observing these subjects' reactions to their trials, and they won't get far.'

Keix didn't know whether she should feel relieved or uneasy at the revelation. *I'm not the only one,* she thought. *Vin must be included in this group too . . .*

'Yes, you keep saying that. But what is so special about them?' Flincon probed. Neither of his colleagues made any discernible move to stop his line of questioning, evident from the long silence that stretched out. Keix supposed that was his purpose in this meeting—voicing rude objections. Suddenly, she didn't think that having so many people listening in on this conversation was such a great idea after all.

'Keix, *together with a select group of others,*' the male Ifarl answered in measured tones, 'seems to have an exceptional level of resilience to torture. She has gone through the whole set of experiments and is still standing. This brings Atros one step closer to their goal of producing a controllable hybrid. She's the only one who *you* know of because Zej was assigned to oversee one—or more—of the experiments on her.'

From the corner of her eye, Keix saw Pod's eyes dart between Zej and her. He was probably trying to determine if the two of them had resolved this issue of Zej being behind the control when she was being drowned and electrocuted, among other things. Pod seemed to let out a breath when he decided that Keix was not going to pursue this matter, at least for now.

What the female Ifarl said next caught everyone's absolute attention. 'Removing Keix from Atros is not enough. Others, like Vin also have the potential to become such hybrids.'

Keix did a double take at the mention of her friend's name even though it only confirmed her suspicions. So, Oka knew all along that Vin was also held at PEER. Was Pod aware of this? His sharp intake of breath indicated that he wasn't privy to the fact and he looked at Zej, who shook his head in affirmation.

'You should have rescued them together. Now that Atros has had a breach in PEER, it's going to be even more difficult to get anyone else out,' added the male Ifarl.

Keix couldn't believe her ears when that Flincon idiot spoke up again. 'Isn't that Vin girl part Ifarl? Why are you getting us to do your dirty work then?' he asked in his offensive way.

The Ifarl elders didn't deign to reply, while protests from both Flincon's colleagues confirmed that he had gone too far with his disrespectful questions this time around.

The mild-mannered voice pointed out that Vin was the only one that was part Ifarl, out of the names the elders had provided them with. The man with the raspy voice told Flincon to take his opinions off the record. But instead of being pacified, Flincon raised his voice and started arguing with both of them. Even without the transmitter, Keix and the rest could hear them in their tiny room.

The racket, combined with the tense atmosphere, caused inexpressible pressure to build up in Keix's head, threatening to burst it open like an overinflated balloon. Before anyone grasped what was happening, she had stormed out of the room and was banging both her fists on the locked door where the meeting was at being held.

'Keix, wait!' Zej and Pod yelled at the same time. Zej swore and came after her. The door clicked open just as he reached her. A bald middle-aged man in a plain grey robe who was around her height stood in front of her. The lack of hair made his sharp features, which were arranged into a look of displeasure, seem even more forbidding. What was more striking, however, was the maze of lines that marked his Ifarl bloodline. Behind him, three figures dressed fully in black were standing, their faces frozen in similar looks of annoyance at having been caught in the middle of their argument.

But Keix's attention was drawn to the oldest-looking woman she had ever set her eyes on. She was seated at the far end of the steel table, dressed similarly to the man who had opened the door. What set her apart was an elaborate and colourful neck-piece made up of an assortment of gemstones, both polished and raw. Keix wondered how the wizened woman could sit up so straight because the accessory looked like it weighed half as much as she did. The old lady's thinning white hair, woven into two neat braids with rainbow-hued threads, barely concealed the maze of red lines that marked her Ifarl ancestry. While the male Ifarl and Vin's markings were pink and Maii's were concealed under a thick head of hair, the old woman's lines were glowing, illuminating the roots of her hair. The pink halo effect underscored her ethereal presence. And she was staring with open curiosity at Keix.

For a moment, with so many pairs of eyes on her, Keix forgot why she had charged into the room. Before she could gather her thoughts, the Ifarl woman spoke. 'You have seen Vin chained up in PEER.'

The statement punctuated the silence and seemed to break everyone out of a spell. The three figures in black resumed speaking at the same time, but the tallest one with the commanding voice spoke the loudest. 'Were you eavesdropping at the door?' he asked without humour. Spotting Zej standing behind Keix, the displeasure in his narrowed eyes deepened. 'I didn't expect this kind of insubordinate behaviour from you, Zej,' he added.

Before Zej could come up with a reply, Keix recovered her composure and said, 'No, I was the one eavesdropping. Zej just found me and was trying to stop me.' There was no way she was going to rat out her friends since she was the one who got them involved in Dace's rebellious act first.

Glad that the rest of them had had the sense to stay away and avoid being implicated, Keix breathed an inward sigh of relief.

The man's expression remained stony.

'I'm sorry, Machillian, sir. I should have kept a better eye on Keix.' Zej squeezed Keix's hand to quiet her objections.

She had a feeling he was trying to defuse the situation with his compliance. Still, she pushed his hand away and raised her voice to take advantage of the temporary silence. 'That is not the point. The point is, yes, I saw Vin in PEER. She was chained up and she looked really frail. We have to get her out, and the rest, if they are there too.' She had no idea who 'the rest' were, but she plunged ahead regardless, adding, 'You cannot allow Atros to carry on their experiments!'

'Now, wait up,' said the one with slicked-back greasy black hair, whose voice Keix recognized as Flincon. He was a short and sturdily built man who looked to be in his late thirties. Short, thin eyebrows like snapped twigs arched over watery eyes gave him an untrustworthy look, adding to Keix's initial dislike of him. 'What we cannot allow is *you* eavesdropping on a high-level meeting!'

The pretty girl standing beside Flincon cleared her throat. She had wavy orange hair that was bundled up into a neat ponytail that reached her waist. Like her voice, she projected an air of collected calm.

Keix had forgotten about the man who opened the door and she almost jumped when he said, 'This young lady is right. In fact, they may have already succeeded in creating a hybrid.'

Everyone turned to face him with gaping mouths, but his grave expression indicated that he was not joking.

'Succeeded?' Keix asked. Seyfer's deranged yellow eyes flashed through her mind, followed by another picture of him with black eyes. Was the Ifarl referring to *him*? Could they read minds? If not, how did the old woman know that she had seen Vin chained up in PEER?

Instead of getting an answer, Machillian raised his voice and said with finality, 'That's enough.' He retrieved a transmitter from his belt and pressed a button. 'Kaplan, please come to the meeting room right now. I need you to escort our guest back to her room and make sure she stays there until I give further instructions.'

Turning to Zej, he added, 'When I am done here, I want to speak to you. Privately. Make sure you're available then.'

Keix paced her room, fuming over the way Kaplan had grabbed her by the arm and dragged her all the way down to the room she had slept in, shoved her in and locked the door. She would have resisted more violently if she had not thought that her friends would be punished for her actions.

Looking around, another surge of anger seized Keix. The windowless room and palm-sized vent would do little to aid her escape. She considered kicking the door down, but the racket would be a dead giveaway. Why hadn't she taken the chance to leave the plant when she could? Now she was stuck. And likely in a worse situation than before. Surely Pod or Zej or even Dace would let her out soon, after Machillian and gang departed? What if Kaplan refused to hand the key over?

A soft click at the door interrupted Keix's mounting agitation. 'Pod?' she called out. But it wasn't her friend, or even Maii, whom she saw when the door cracked open. In fact, it was the last person on earth she would have imagined seeing there—the Ifarl woman.

Up close, the elderly Ifarl's eyes seemed to be changing shades constantly, from a deep sea blue to a light sky blue and back. Keix stood there, transfixed, and at a loss as to what to say.

'Hi, Keix,' the old woman said with a smile that crinkled up her deeply lined face even more.

'Erm . . . How did . . .Why . . .What . . .' Keix stuttered.

Gesturing to the inside of Keix's prison, the Ifarl asked, 'May I? I would very much prefer that we keep the forthcoming conversation strictly between the two of us.'

A bewildered Keix stepped back to let the Ifarl into the room. The old woman proceeded to perch on the unmade bed to make herself comfortable. Perhaps due to the powerful aura with which she carried herself, Keix felt a little diminished in the elder's presence.

After Keix closed the door, the Ifarl spoke. 'My name is Zenchi, and I am *a friend.*'

Keix paused in her tracks. The intonation with which Zenchi said the last two words couldn't have been a mere coincidence.

'I know you have your doubts, but I am here to tell you that Oka will not help you in your attempt to retrieve Vin from Atros,' continued Zenchi. 'They are too obsessed with the "big picture" to realize that the key to gaining the upper hand in a war is, more often than not, to win small battles. Small, but significant.'

It took Keix a few seconds to find her voice. 'But aren't Ifarls too, concerned with the big picture? Your comrade said so himself. That you do not engage in these frivolous battles.'

A soft musical laughter filled the air. 'Wakei is young. He has yet to grasp the nuances of what frivolousness is. Regardless,' Zenchi said airily, 'the act of saving Vin will further undermine Atros's efforts to gain a ghostly army headed by hybrid generals. And by hybrids, I mean humans who have been possessed.'

'By ghosts?' Keix croaked.

It was a silly and redundant question, but there was no trace of scorn in Zenchi's nod. She elaborated, 'The conditions of the possession process are strictly monitored to ensure the bonding of the souls. Once that is done, the person straddles both realms, allowing them to communicate with beings in each of them.'

'Am I . . . one of them? Is that why I can . . . *touch* them?' whispered Keix.

'Not yet,' replied Zenchi. 'Your transition isn't complete.'

At these words, something Seyfer said during their run-in popped into Keix's mind. *Tell me, how did your friends know where you were? And to rescue you the day before you were scheduled for your sentence?* he had asked. Was this 'sentence' he had been talking about the same as the possession that Zenchi mentioned? If Zej and Pod had not broken her out, would she have become like Seyfer? She shivered at the thought.

'How do you know this? Have you told Oka—that Machillian guy?' Keix asked.

'Not about you. But yes, they know about this hybridization process, as you've undoubtedly heard,' replied Zenchi, referring to their earlier encounter. 'But Oka doesn't believe in acting without concrete knowledge. This is the main reason why only you were retrieved from PEER. Right now, the tides have shifted. The advantage of a blind strike is lost. But you can still do it. Bring your friends, Zej, Pod, Maii and Dace. You will not succeed in this task if you attempt it alone.'

'Maii is not my friend. She's one of you.' Once the words were out of her mouth, Keix wished she hadn't let slip her dislike of Maii.

Zenchi gave her a knowing smile. 'Maii is with Pod. She'll go if he goes. Her presence will only add to your advantage.'

Damn right it will, thought Keix. Maii's mind-control abilities would come in handy. The only thing was that she was a weapon that Keix had no idea how to wield. Which made her about as dangerous as an army of Odats—or even more so.

Keix chose her next words carefully. She didn't want to mention Maii again even though the damage was done. She wondered why Zenchi brought up Dace. 'How can you be sure that they will back me up?'

'Everyone has their own agenda,' Zenchi didn't supplement her statement.

Keix suddenly felt that surge of resentment all over again. 'You know, Flincon was right. If this is so important to you, why not gather your Ifarls and launch a rescue? Why are you getting others like Oka—or me, even—to do your dirty work for you?'

Zenchi stood up from the bed and stretched her hands towards Keix. At the swiftness of the old woman's movement, Keix jumped back, trying to avoid the reach of those wizened hands, which looked like they belonged on a corpse. Considering the size of the room, the manoeuvre wasn't really easy to achieve. But Keix didn't want to test her strength on a full-out Ifarl elder, especially not when the old woman was the frailest-looking person she had ever seen. 'What are you doing?' she asked, trying to keep the panic out of her voice.

'Will you trust *a friend*?' Zenchi's eyes twinkled, turning a deep indigo.

Keix frowned, but she stopped retreating. Zenchi's words played a part in this, but the other part was the fact that she had nowhere else to retreat to unless she were to get out of the room.

'Let me show you,' Zenchi said, reaching her spidery fingers to Keix's face.

With great restraint, Keix managed to keep her body still and her breathing even although her instincts were screaming at her to run. She flinched when the Ifarl elder touched her temples. At the contact, Zenchi started humming a low tune. The air in the room stirred, buzzing with an unseen intensity. Keix didn't understand the words the elder was singing, but even an idiot could tell that there was magic in them, woven together with the melody, creating a force she had never seen nor felt before. Coaxed by Zenchi's powers, Keix felt a gradual familiar warmth kindling at the back of her brain. The glow grew as the music picked up. When the Ifarl intoned the last note, Keix knew without a doubt that the well of energy that had swelled within her was now possibly bottomless.

Mission accomplished, Zenchi removed her fingers from Keix and said, 'You might want to tell your friends about this. Wouldn't want to shock them in battle,' she said.

Keix reached her hands to where Zenchi had placed her fingers. 'What did you just do?' she couldn't keep the awe, shock and fear out of her voice.

Zenchi's reply was another enigmatic smile before she swept out of the room. Keix didn't bother to try the door after it closed behind the Ifarl with a soft click because she was sure it was locked once again. She sat down on the bed, dumbfounded. Her mind was blank except for that reserve of power the Ifarl had just unlocked.

Keix didn't know how much time had passed since Zenchi had gone. But after she had gathered her wits, she tried to access the buzzing glow, shaping and moulding it in various ways. The only problem was that there was nothing for her to test her power on. Just as she was running out of patience, darkness engulfed the room. The low whirr of the ventilation system went silent. Right on cue, a stale smell crept into her surroundings. Keix tried the doorknob but it was still locked. She pulled harder, using her body weight to try to force the door open to no avail. She placed her ear flat against the door. Nothing. After several moments, an idea struck her. She drew on the well of energy at the back of her head and channelled it into her shoulder.

'Here goes nothing,' she muttered, ramming into the door. It splintered like a flimsy matchstick and swung off its hinges. The sudden momentum pitched Keix forward and she felt the door colliding with something on the other side.

'Ow!'

Keix recognized the voice. 'Maii?' she asked, incredulous.

'I thought the door opened inwards?'

The hallway outside wasn't as dark as the room. In the soft glow from the ends of the corridor, Keix saw Maii rubbing her shoulder.

'What are you doing here?'

'Questions later. Come with me first,' replied Maii, enclosing Keix's wrist in a vice-like grip and tugging her along the corridor.

Keix tried to shake Maii off when she recalled Zenchi's 'advice'. She couldn't help but suspect that Maii had been sent on the Ifarl elder's orders to keep an eye on her.

'Where the hell do you think you are taking me?' Keix didn't try to keep the anger out of her voice. She dug her feet harder into the ground.

The sound of footsteps pressed pause on Keix and Maii's struggle. Pod was running over from the end of the hallway which led to the control room. He skidded to a stop when he saw the broken door. 'I thought the door opened inwards?' he asked.

'We haven't got time for this, Pod,' hissed Maii.

'Oh, right,' said Pod.

Keix could literally see him putting his thoughts on reverse.

'Sh—Oh, no. Oh, no! We've got to go, Keix. Now!' said Pod, grabbing her free arm.

Before she knew what was happening, Keix was sandwiched between Pod and Maii, who were dragging her along the corridor. Both of them spoke at the same time.

'We're under attack—'

'We've got to get—*What*?' Maii interrupted herself mid-sentence at Pod's words.

'There's a group of soldiers, likely Atros-trained, sweeping through the facility right now. Machillian received a tip-off just now and we were supposed to evacuate. But they came right at us before we could do anything.'

Keix stopped resisting and the three of them broke into a run.

'Maii was supposed to get you and transport you to another facility—'

'*But*,' Maii continued in a louder voice before Keix could protest, 'we're not going to do that.'

Keix's brows snapped together. 'Really?'

Ignoring her sarcasm, Pod answered in an even tone. 'We're going to get you out of here. Look, Keix, eavesdropping on that meeting was a great idea. None of us were aware that the Ifarl elders have warned Oka that others had to be rescued. Hell, we didn't even know that Oka was communicating with the Ifarls. All my digging in PEER's files—and never once did Vin's name come up. And Zej said you told him that you saw her when you went into the vent during your escape. Why didn't you tell me earlier?' Pod sounded genuinely hurt.

'How did I know I could trust you guys again? After you straight out told me that you had joined a rebel group.'

'I joined Oka to save you! And I told Zej it was a bad idea to tell you from the get-go about that . . .' murmured Pod.

Before Keix could give Pod a piece of her mind, two helmeted figures stepped into view. She rushed forward and slammed her fist into one of them. The person gave a grunt at the impact and returned a punch, which she sidestepped, before reaching out and peeling off her attacker's head gear. In one swift move, she slammed his head against the wall. The figure fell to the floor without another sound.

Keix turned back to see the other soldier grappling with Maii and Pod. This trooper was taller and larger built than his associate. He was also more agile, ducking and attacking without effort despite the limited amount of space. Even so, he was outnumbered and Maii and Pod managed to strip off his helmet. Keix took advantage of the opening to swing the head gear she had picked up from her earlier fight towards the back of the man's head. With a loud crunch, he was knocked unconscious too.

Pod stepped over the body and hurried on, 'We're meeting Zej at the gate. We'll make use of this chance to disappear from both Atros and Oka's radars. Brilliant, eh?'

'Disappear?' Keix asked, keeping up with him.

'Yeah! We'll pretend to be caught by these Atros soldiers,' said Pod, gesturing to the bodies.

'How do you know they're from Atros?'

Pod turned to Keix and gave her a look of disbelief. She and Maii almost ran into him at the sudden stop.

'The story's not going to hold up when Oka's spies find out that we weren't captured,' insisted Keix.

'We'll be in hiding by then. It won't matter.'

'Then we'd have two organizations chasing after us!'

Pod dared to give her an exasperated sigh. 'Are you saying you would prefer that we followed orders and bring you back to Oka?'

'No way!'

'Then we're sticking to my more brilliant plan, of course.'

'No. I meant . . . you could let me go, then tell Oka that I escaped in the chaos. I don't want to implicate you guys any more than I already have.'

Zenchi's words replayed in Keix's head at her objections. *You will not succeed in this task if you attempt it alone.*

'Yeah, like we're going to do that,' said Pod. 'We're too far in. We're sticking with you regardless. To go into hiding for an unauthorized mission—to save *your* best friend, mind you—or back to Oka's facility. It's your choice.'

'Enough,' Maii interrupted.

Keix had almost forgotten her presence while bickering with Pod.

'It doesn't matter what you say, Keix. We're sticking to the escape plan. Spiral steps ahead. Let's go.'

They had reached the landing of the steps just outside the control room. A dim beam of light was shining down the spiral staircase, whose first steps Maii had already mounted. Pod waved a hand to ask Keix to get going, and she hesitated for a moment before complying. She was surprised that Maii had not charmed her into collaborating with them. For a moment, she considered running away from Pod and Maii once they reached the surface. But there was no denying that she needed help if she wanted to get Vin—and more people—out of PEER. Even without Zenchi and Oron's urging, the chances of her walking into any Atros facility without drawing attention was next to zero given her current 'Wanted' status. With that thought, she climbed up the stairs behind Maii and heard Pod mutter in relief.

Despite the fact that she knew they were under attack, Keix had assumed that the fight would be on a small scale. After all, if Atros had enough intel to launch an attack within such short notice, they would probably be aware that there was barely anyone in the facility—besides the three of them, Keix had only seen Zej, Dace and Kaplan so far. But when she reached the top of the stairs, she realized that Atros had decided to take the concept of overkill to the next level.

Under the cloudy night sky, in the open space right in front of the door, almost three dozen enemies, half of which were Odats, were circling Dace and Zej.

11

Plans and Craziness

Keix sprang into action. She took out two of the soldiers nearest to her before the group even realized that they were now facing five people instead of two.

Maii and Pod joined the fray, each wrestling with a trooper. Zej was holding his own against an Odat that was trying to knock him out. The rest of the creatures seemed to be holding back, but in the temporary confusion, two of them had managed to grab Dace and were twisting his arms to his back. Keix jumped at one of them, harnessing a jolt of power from the back of her mind and directing it to her foot as she landed a kick at its shoulder. At the contact, the Odat flew back and slammed into the fence. Keix saw the hesitation in its comrade's eyes as she turned towards it.

Too bad, smirked Keix. The delay allowed her to hit the Odat's head. It let go of its hostage and staggered back at the impact. With a series of power-infused punches, she knocked this one out too.

Casting a glance around, Keix wondered if Seyfer was heading this group. The uniforms looked right, but none of them looked tall enough. A grunt interrupted her thoughts. Zej had dispatched his Odat. Dace, Pod and Maii were now engaged in fist fights with the other soldiers. No weapons were in sight. Keix surmised that the group was probably ordered to capture everyone alive and did a quick count. Three troopers to each of them. It wasn't bad odds. She just needed to help keep the Odats' attention on her since these ones seemed to follow herd mentality. She scanned their faces. Even though she wasn't an expert in reading their expressions, she could tell by the way their eyes swivelled between her and her friends that they were debating whether they should take out the weaker links or neutralize the bigger threat. She rushed towards another Odat and flung it against the fence. The rest of the creatures turned to her, their decision made.

Keix fought back an involuntary hint of panic as they swarmed at her. It had been tough fighting one of these bloodthirsty creatures when she was weakened back at PEER. Her newfound power had tipped the scales in her favour. But with a mob of them, things became a little more complicated. Keix soon realized that sustained use of her new energy required more of her strength than she had anticipated.

Sweat poured down her back as she aimed punch after punch, kick after kick, at her aggressors. The brutes closed in on her, attacking in waves from all directions. With every Odat that fell, Keix backed up another step against the fence. If she could get them all in front of her, she would waste less energy turning to fend them off.

Keix tried to pace her laboured breaths. She thanked her lucky stars for the crisp night air, which invigorated her senses as she knocked another Odat off its feet.

Three more to go, she told herself.

As the thought crossed her mind, she heard Pod shout, 'Hey, you!'

One of the Odats turned towards the sound. Wrong move. Zej and Pod pounced on it in a coordinated attack while Dace brought two helmets together like cymbals, striking the creature's head and rendering it unconscious.

Keix bent down and kicked at one of the other brute's knees. It howled in pain and lunged at her. Only when its hands closed around her neck did she realize that she had misjudged the distance. She clawed at the creature's chunky fingers as she kicked at it. Stars were appearing in her vision and the glowing well of power was receding out of reach. As Keix gasped for air, the Odat uttered, 'Tear. Limb. From. Limb.'

'Sure, knock yourself out,' Maii's melodious voice said in reply.

The spell, though not directed at Keix, penetrated the haze obscuring her sight. She felt the Odat's grip loosen and her eyes focused just in time to see the brute punch itself in the head before falling onto her.

Keix would have laughed if she hadn't just had the wind knocked out of her or if her throat wasn't raw and achy. Still, she managed a word of thanks as Dace and Pod pulled the unconscious Odat off her and helped her up.

Making their way back to the gate, Keix and the rest only encountered minor scuffles. They helped dispatch a couple of soldiers who were carrying off an unconscious Kaplan, before hiding him in a darkened corner. Machillian, Flincon and the orange-haired woman were nowhere in sight.

As they approached the main gate, Keix saw a group of people gathered at the security post. From the looks of it, these individuals had nothing to do with Oka.

'Not here,' said Dace. He put a hand on Keix's shoulders and looked at the rest. 'There's no way we're going to get a car and drive out of that mess without attracting attention.'

'You've got a better idea?' asked Pod.

'I've got a better ride.'

Dace led the group away from the plant towards the forest. Minutes after they entered the thicket, Dace felt around purposefully and gave a triumphant smile as his hands closed around something in the air. With a flourish, he pulled off what Keix presumed was an invisibility 'cape' of sorts to reveal a sleek black five-seater hovercar.

Pod's jaw dropped. Maii looked surprised. Even Zej looked grudgingly impressed at the reveal.

'So . . . where to now?' Dace's question was directed at Keix.

'As far from the sectors as possible, of course,' answered Pod, recovering his composure.

'No,' interrupted Keix, to everyone's astonishment. 'We head to PEER.'

'Are you mad?' That was Pod. 'We barely escaped them and now you want to dive back into the jaws of death? Without a plan?'

Keix ignored Pod's melodramatic reaction. 'Everything's been put on turbo mode since you guys rescued me from PEER. We've got to stop Atros before they get their army of hybrids. Which means we've got to do it sooner than later.' She recapped her encounter with Seyfer, which did little to allay the look of disbelief on Pod's face.

'Look, you don't have to come with me,' continued Keix.

'Well, we're not letting you do this on your own,' Zej addressed Keix, but he was looking at Pod.

'Of course, we're not letting her go on her own,' retorted Pod, offended. 'I wasn't objecting to the mission per se. Just the lack of a proper plan.' He looked to Maii, who returned a curt nod.

'Well, whatever it is, we need to get out of here fast,' Dace cut in, opening the door to the car. He gestured to the horizon and added, 'Because we'd need to outrun whatever that is—and I'm assuming it's nothing good.'

Everyone looked towards the direction he was pointing at. A multi-coloured glow was just about visible, moving fast. It could only mean one thing. Ghosts.

The atmosphere inside the car was tense as Dace drove. Maii was riding shotgun.

'You'll need me to convince anyone who comes across us to leave us alone,' she had reasoned. Which meant that Keix had ended up being sandwiched between Pod and Zej at the back.

Pod began laying out plans for the rescue. 'Safe house. Disguises. Weapons. A debrief. In that order,' he concluded.

'I can get us to a safe house,' replied Dace. 'It's at the other end of Sector L, though. So we'll need to get past the guards and through the sector without drawing attention to ourselves.'

No one raised any objections because the glow behind them seemed to draw nearer with every passing minute. Once, Dace had to take a detour to avoid the coloured mist for fear that the ghosts would affect the engines. The second time, they actually had to hide to let the cloud of spectres overtake them.

Keix had protested against leading the ghosts towards the sector, but Dace had pointed out that the troopers at Sector L were better equipped than the five of them to take on the apparitions. 'And they only have to hold them off until sunrise,' he added. Keix looked around. Sure enough, the sun was rising, which meant that the ghosts would scatter and not regroup until sundown.

Even though the decision was the most practical one, Keix was not prepared for the sight that greeted them at the sector border. Warm, morning light bathed the area, dispelling the chill of the night. It also highlighted the bodies of Atros soldiers strewn about. Cars and hovercars were scattered everywhere. Backup and first-aid troopers rushed around, tending to the injured. Groans could be heard even as Dace manoeuvred the hovercar to a more deserted stretch of land. In the chaos, no one even thought to stop or inspect their car.

Past the border, Keix saw more traces of the ghostly attack. Civilians were helping to move those who were lying unconscious by the pavements and roadside. Cars which had collided into each other or into lamp posts sat abandoned.

But Dace was right. The disastrous effect of the attack had been minimized because the sector had a first line of defence in the form of Atros soldiers. Still, that did little to ease Keix's guilt. Everyone's faces remained solemn even when they reached their destination.

The safe house turned out to be a cosy five-bedroom bungalow by a body of water. Concealed behind overgrown hedges that had blended seamlessly into the cluster of trees, it definitely wasn't a place anyone would chance upon by accident. Its sprawling grounds still retained an air of opulence despite the obvious fact that it had been neglected for a long time.

'This house used to belong to a rich eccentric couple,' explained Dace as he stepped out of the hovercar. 'They passed away about a decade ago, and their only son doesn't bother with the upkeep of the place because he prefers the city life. We should be safe here for the moment.'

Keix wondered how Dace was related to this 'son' but she kept her thoughts to herself.

After some discussion, Dace set off with Maii to go into the neighbouring Sector G to obtain disguises and food. Pod disappeared into one of the rooms, muttering something about drawing up a more concrete plan. Zej sagged down on the armchair in the living room and closed his eyes.

Left to her own devices, Keix decided to explore the rest of the house. Besides the furniture, everything else that could give any indication of who the owners were, such as personal effects and photos, had been removed. Two of the rooms she came across had identical four-poster beds and dressers. The third was a study which had a handsome mahogany desk in the middle of it, surrounded by floor-to-ceiling shelves of the same colour. A thick layer of dust had settled over all the exposed surfaces, including the vast number of books that the shelves held. Pushing open the doors to an adjoining balcony, Keix breathed in the fresh smell of salt mingled with that of an old library.

The sun was hanging high in the sky now, casting specks of gold on the light blue water. The view might have been breathtaking if not for the memories it evoked—the underwater cavern, the heart-clenching betrayal of Atros, of Zej . . .

Wrenching herself out of these dark reflections, she played out in her mind the various actions they could take to rescue Vin. Footsteps sounded at the door and Keix pivoted on the spot just in time to see Pod popping his head into the room.

'Hey . . .' Pod began. 'I was wondering if you wanted to . . . you know, talk.' He stepped in and closed the door behind him.

Keix raised an eyebrow at Pod. 'About the plan?'

Pod shook his head. 'No, I mean . . . yes, we need to talk about the plan. But that can wait. Till Dace and Maii get back. I . . .' He took a deep breath before launching ahead. 'I just wanted to know if you and Zej are cool? Because you know, when he came to me after he oversaw your torture, he seemed to have lost it. Really. And since then, I was with Zej every time he met with Machillian—

he was the one who recruited Zej. He fought so hard to try to get Machillian to provide a safe house and the necessary equipment, like high-tech jamming signals and the control table so we could get you out. I didn't place much faith in Oka, even though I always had the feeling that Machillian had a soft spot for Zej. I guess I was wrong,' he added with a shrug.

Keix took a moment to consider Pod's question. Sure, she had been upset when she first found out about Zej's betrayal, but she also understood that it wasn't like he had had any choice in that matter. Besides, if they had really got her out just a day before she was scheduled to be 'sentenced'— whatever that entailed—she ought to be nothing but grateful to them. She shrugged by way of answer.

'Do you still trust Zej?'

Keix thought about it. 'Yes.'

'Do you trust his judgement?'

An image of Machillian popped into her head. 'I . . . guess so.'

Pod heaved an exaggerated sigh of relief.

'How about Maii?' asked Keix, catching him off guard.

'Maii? What about Maii?'

'What's her story? Why did she join Oka?'

Pod hesitated. 'I've been trying to find out too, but she's quite tight-lipped about that. Do you think she's a spy for the Ifarls?'

Keix nodded and then said after pondering for a moment, 'You know, you're pretty much useless. And here I thought you knew her so well because you're always hanging around her.'

To Keix's surprise, Pod gave her a sheepish look instead of one of his witty retorts. 'Well,' he began, 'it's not like I'm not trying.'

Something in his tone made Keix study him a little more intently. She saw a flush creeping up his neck. It took a while before the implication of his bashful behaviour dawned on her. 'You have a crush on her, don't you?' Keix said, laughing. As far as she knew, Pod had never expressed interest in any girls before.

Pod gave Keix an exasperated look, but he didn't refute her. He was spared the need to explain himself when a shout from the living room interrupted their discussion. 'We're back! With food and disguises!' came Dace's voice.

Stepping into the living room, Keix did a double take. Dace was decked out in an expensive-looking leather jacket, dark jeans and high-top boots. The swagger that had previously felt strangely out of place with his baggy, mangy clothes and flip-flops now seemed to fit its owner like a bespoke suit.

Dace gave a hearty laugh at her surprise. 'Who would have known that I'd clean up better than you, huh, Keix?' he joked while he spread out several boxes of pizza on the dusty glass coffee table.

Keix pretended she couldn't hear him. She couldn't help but steal a glance at Maii in light of Pod's recent confession. The Ifarl was her usual silent self. Leaning against the stone mantelpiece, she looked like she was posing for one of those fashionable advertisements commonly flashed on electronic billboards in the malls. While Dace had done a complete one-eighty-degree turn with his outfit. Maii was still dressed in her head-to-toe black leather ensemble. Keix wondered if she had had anything to do with Dace's new threads; the two of them would have no trouble passing off as style twins.

Dace rummaged through the bag and retrieved a long pink wig. 'For you,' he said to Keix.

'What? Wouldn't I draw more attention with this hair?' she asked in disbelief.

'Not according to Maii,' Dace said with a shrug. He placed it on the table since Keix refused to take it from him.

Without inflection, Maii said, 'This is the most popular hairstyle now. Six out of ten people were wearing this at the mall, men included. Be thankful I managed to snag one of the last pieces.'

Keix saw Pod trying to hide a smile behind his pizza. She couldn't refute the logic behind what Maii said, so she said instead, 'Zej also wanted one. He should get one too.'

'He will,' Dace cut in, pulling out another pink wig from the bag. This was shorter though, and in a darker shade. 'I'll leave it to you to fight it out,' he added, tossing it to Keix.

Pod choked on his drink, while Zej gave a resigned look and picked up the long wig.

'Both of you should put them on, so we know if these disguises work,' Pod said as soon as he stopped sputtering.

Keix expected Zej to object, so she was shocked when he put on the hairpiece and gave an exaggerated hair flip which made everyone, including Dace, laugh. The colour of the hair clashed with Zej's stubble; Keix had a feeling that it wouldn't look so bizarre once he had shaved. Pulling hers on without further complaint, Keix checked her reflection in the mirror above the mantelpiece. The bright hair made her skin look less sallow in contrast, and she was sure that, with some heavy make-up, she would look quite different to those who didn't know her that well.

Dace passed them each a bag of new clothes while they finished up the food. 'Maii bought them, so you can go to her if you have any issues with them,' he said, before turning to Pod and adding, 'So what's the plan?'

The mood, which had lightened considerably, turned grave once more as Pod cleared his throat. 'I hate to break it to you, but there's no way the five of us are going to sneak into PEER. But,' he added in a hurry, 'I have a plan. And it involves both of you—' he gestured to Keix and Zej '— getting caught by Atros.'

As Pod detailed his plan, it soon became apparent that having Keix and Zej caught was the least preposterous part of it.

'There's an underground club in Sector L that Atros's soldiers frequent,' began Pod. 'Keix and Zej will head there in disguise tonight and we will tip-off Atros. After the troopers arrest them, Dace, Maii and I will follow at a safe distance until we reach the city centre. We'll ambush the vehicle once we get near PEER and Maii will "convince" them to let us in. Once I get into the control room at PEER, I'll set off all the alarms and mayhem will ensue. We can take the chance then to find Vin and get her out before anyone notices. Of course, we'll all be carrying trackers so we know where everyone else is at all times. And we'll meet at a fixed rendezvous point once we've grabbed Vin.'

Keix stared at him slack-jawed. 'There are so many things that could go wrong! What if Atros decides not to take us to PEER?'

'Well, we can't exactly go knocking on the front door of PEER asking to be let in, right? The last time we were there to get you out, I had a proper control table and high-tech jamming signals courtesy of Oka. Right now, the only way to hack the system is from the inside. So I need to get into the control room there. Plus, not to mention, we also had Zej's authorized pass then. Now, he's on the "Wanted" list,' reasoned Pod.

'What about the ghost attack last night? Wouldn't Atros or anyone at all be on higher alert? Going to a club should be their lowest priority right now, shouldn't it? And what if they send too many soldiers for us to handle?' protested Keix.

'Not if they want to maintain a semblance of normality,' interjected Dace. 'Atros is downplaying the attack and saying they've got everything contained. They also said they would increase patrols at the borders, which means fewer soldiers to deploy for ad hoc missions. It was all over the news when Maii and I were at the mall.'

'There you go,' said Pod, as if that settled everything.

Several more rounds of argument later, they settled on a modified version of Pod's plan. The five of them were going to the club to suss out the situation first. If Dace's deduction that Atros had fewer troops to deploy after last night's ghost attack proved right, they would proceed with getting caught. And the tip-off would be for someone low enough on the 'Wanted' list to avoid getting mobbed, but high enough to warrant them to be sent to PEER.

'At the first sign of trouble, I want you guys to run and hide. Regroup. Go to Oka or approach the Ifarls. But don't ever engage Atros. Especially not if Seyfer's heading the group, okay?' stressed Keix. Following tense murmurs of agreement from the rest, she decided to come clean with these people who were willingly following her into what was likely a suicide mission, 'And there's something you need to know. I know it sounds crazy, but . . . I can fight ghosts.'

Everyone seemed struck dumb for a second following her declaration. Then Pod let out a snort of laughter. Dace looked amused. Zej and Maii were looking at her with their brows furrowed.

Zej spoke first, 'You mean you've fought them before?'

Keix nodded, recounting how Seyfer had unleashed the spectres on her. 'When I found you after you fell off your hoverboard on the way to the hut, you were being attacked by three of them. I don't think those were the same ones Seyfer commanded, though,' she replied. 'And Zenchi, the Ifarl elder who was in the Oka meeting, came to my room afterwards. She did something to unlock that well of power. Previously, I could only access it when I was panicked or in extreme pain when I came into contact with ghosts. Now, I can channel that energy when I fight. And it's not just being able to hit paranormal beings—my strength multiplies too.'

'Is that how you managed to take down all those Odats?' asked Pod, still grappling with her latest revelation.

Keix nodded.

'And here I thought it was just the legendary Kulcan strength at work,' he continued.

Maii's next sentence caught everyone by surprise. 'You should pace yourself.'

Of all the heads that turned towards her, Pod's eyes and mouth were opened the widest. 'What? You've known this all along?'

Keix saw Maii's eyes soften when she looked at Pod and explained, 'I didn't. But it would figure that one can only cross the threshold between life and death so many times before he or she becomes connected to both worlds. The tortures Keix was put through at PEER . . . how many times had she been on the verge of dying before being brought back? And we heard the elders during the meeting. Hybrids that straddle the worlds of the living and the dead—I think with a little imagination, we can all make pretty good guesses as to how they are formed.' To Keix, she added, 'if an Ifarl elder has unlocked the ability in you to be the link between these two, without you being possessed by a ghost, it means you are wielding a foreign strength. And that is bound to take a toll on your body. Even Ifarls, who are born into their power, don't go about achieving their goals by "mind-controlling" everyone.'

Keix was taken aback by Maii's little speech. It was the most she had ever heard her speak. She had also never thought that she would see the day when the Ifarl would volunteer advice or divulge any type of information to her kind.

'Well, I'm not worried about you turning translucent and going all berserk on us,' declared Pod in that off-handed way of his, as if his previous eye-bulging moment had not occurred. 'You're still the Keix I know—weird power or not. And the best thing? You're on our side and we're on yours. Ergo, we're on the same side. So, it'll be nothing but advantageous for us if we get attacked by Atros's ghost troops—or any random apparition for that matter. Right, Zej?'

Zej's expression was closed, but he nodded at Pod's words.

'Well, well, well,' Dace said loudly, clapping his hands. 'Now that we've established that we're one big happy family, I think it's time we take a little timeout from this group bonding thing and get some rest before the big night tonight, ya? I, for one, am dead tired from being an errand boy.' He stood up and stretched his arms above his head, letting out a huge yawn. 'And for the record, I don't think you're crazy. A little unstable though. Maybe,' he added to Keix, chucking her under the chin. 'But not crazy, if that wasn't clear when I didn't laugh at or question your declaration.'

12

Unexpected Guests

'May I?' asked Keix.

Dace, who was sitting in the high-backed chair behind the desk, looked up and waved her in.

'You sure you don't need to rest? You look exhausted,' said Dace, breaking the awkward silence. At Keix's half-shrug, he sighed. 'All right, shoot. I know you have questions.'

Keix was reminded of her first conversation with Dace. There was a straightforwardness to him that made Keix trust him implicitly. She thought for a moment before deciding to go straight to the point. 'Why are you here?'

'Because this is my house?' he gave a wry smile.

The admission surprised Keix, but she refused to let that derail her line of questioning. 'I mean, why are you getting involved in all this? You don't have the same obligations as Zej and Pod. You hardly know us.'

'The same can be said of Maii.'

Keix thought about Zenchi's words. 'Maii is . . . a different story.'

Dace raised his eyebrow. 'Yeah, her Ifarl powers are of more help to you while I'm just a useless warm body tagging along.'

Keix could tell he was pretending to be offended. Still, she clarified, 'That's not what I'm saying!'

'Well, maybe I'm just looking to rebel against the rebels. Helping you fits the bill.'

Keix narrowed her eyes at him.

'All right, I cave. Your ability to tell when I'm hedging is uncanny.' With a grin, he added, 'You might be my soulmate, you know?'

'You can't sweet talk me, Dace. Tell me, why exactly are you here? With us?'

Dace let out a long breath. 'You know how I feel about orders?'

Keix nodded. Orders are not so much orders to me as they are guidelines, he had said.

'Well, Machillian had a daughter. Her name was Lana,' Dace began, his eyes growing wistful. 'I met her when I first joined Oka. I just wanted to be on a different side than Atros because . . .' he let the sentence hang but Keix didn't press for an explanation.

'Lana was graceful and mature. And she had this natural wit that really intrigued me. We . . . grew close. I guess you could say that we were together, if you really wanted to put a label on it.

'Then two years ago, Lana, me and two others were tasked with stealing some equipment from the Atros camp in Sector G. It was supposed to be an easy grab-and-go mission. But Atros had stepped up the patrols. We didn't

know. Some troopers spotted us and we got into a fight. I
called for backup, then I realized that they had got Lana.

'And suddenly, out of nowhere, came this small swarm
of ghosts. They attacked the Atros troops, but I was spared
because I was a certain distance away. Machillian ordered
me to use the black hole rounds. He insisted on it even
after I told him that Lana had been captured by Atros and
was within the effective range of the bullet.'

Two years ago, thought Keix. She wondered if it was
just before the Sector L incident, because she recalled
that Oron had said during their briefing that paranormal
activities and enemy raids had been increasing in frequency
in the past months. An image of Vin surrounded by glowing
orbs and translucent beings came to Keix. She understood
Dace's dilemma.

'I couldn't pull the trigger.' Anguish and bitterness
was apparent in every word. 'And I would have gone
back for her if Zej hadn't appeared. He fired without
hesitation and pulled me away. For disobeying orders, I
was put out of active duty, relegated to looking at screens
at the stupid plant.'

It wasn't a good time to defend Zej, but Keix was
sure that when he had fired the black hole bullet, he was
aware that the suction would only transport them to an
Atros facility. But then again, it didn't seem particularly
comforting to tell Dace that Zej might have placed Lana in
a situation where she might have been subject to the same
torture Keix herself had gone through. It would sound even
worse if Keix mentioned the possibility that Lana might
have been turned into a hybrid like Seyfer.

Dace had lapsed into deep thought, so Keix chose her next words carefully. 'What if,' she said tentatively, '—and that's a big *if*—if I told you that those swallowed by black hole bullets may not have disappeared forever?'

At her words, Dace's head snapped up. 'What do you mean?'

'I was in the same situation as you when Sector L was attacked. I fired a black hole bullet and Vin, my best friend—the one we're on our way to rescue—was sucked in.' Hope rekindled in Dace's eyes as Keix explained how the bullets actually created a portal to another Atros facility instead of sending people to, well, a black hole like everyone had always assumed.

'You're not saying this just to comfort me, right?' Dace asked, then his expression grew solemn. 'Then it means that Atros might be torturing her!'

Keix placed her hand on Dace's shoulder. 'We don't know for sure. But we're getting everyone out from PEER. Every. Single. One. I'll get Pod to keep a lookout for Lana too. She's as much a priority as Vin. I promise.'

Covering Keix's hand with his own, Dace didn't utter a word. But his gratitude was conveyed through the warmth of his palm, which made hers tingle a little.

Forget the style twins. As they stood together in the garage, the five of them now looked like style quintuplets who had taken their love for leather way overboard. Pod had coloured his ash red hair black, but kept the curls. Zej and Keix were wearing the pink wigs. Only Maii's and Dace's hair remained unchanged, hers pink and straight, and his ginger and curly. Since Zej and Dace seemed unfazed by their makeovers, Keix decided to keep her opinions to herself. She looked down at her outfit. Her jacket ended a little above her hip and had cone-shaped rivets all around the bottom hem and the cuffs. Under it, she wore a loose fit T-shirt which was tucked into a pair of stretchable skinny jeans that fit her perfectly. Even the heavy-duty boots laced up to her calves were comfortable despite the fact that they had never been broken in. With kohl heavily lining her eyes and the pink wig, Keix didn't think that anyone would recognize her even if they were looking closely at her.

Dace parked the hovercar three blocks from the underground club and they split up into two groups. Keix and Zej were supposed to enter the club first to assess the situation. In the meantime, Dace, Pod and Maii were going to wait for their signal, which would indicate that they should proceed with their original plan while keeping an eye out for any sign of Atros outside the club.

Keix and Zej got past the bouncers without a hitch. Once inside, Keix saw that Dace and Pod's assumptions had been right. A party was in full swing. Music was hammering from speakers as large as half a car, threatening to bring the walls down with each subsequent beat. The dance floor was packed with gyrating bodies and the smell of sweat, alcohol and perfumes, both cheap and expensive, clung to the air.

Maii's insistence on the popularity of the wigs and the style of the clothes she picked out were spot-on. It was as if someone had taken the five of them standing in the garage earlier and replicated it hundreds of times over in this space. With everyone mashed together and the spinning overhead rainbow lights, it was hard to keep track of someone, much less navigate from one side of the room to another.

Zej must have had the same thought because he reached for her hand and looped his fingers through hers. They tried their best to fit in, swaying their bodies to the music while subtly making their way across the room. At a tug from Zej, Keix looked up. He held up a phone and pointed to the other corner of the room. Keix nodded in response. Even though they were only inches apart, any attempt at talking would have been drowned out by the deafening music. She took the phone from Zej and read the message that he had typed out to the rest.

Full house in the club.

Pod's reply: *Plan a go?*

Keix typed: *Five more minutes. Need to make sure nothing's amiss.*

Pod's reply was almost immediate. *Paranoid.*

Keix tapped Zej's shoulder and gestured to the bar. It was elevated, providing a better vantage point. She gestured for Zej to bend down. 'Let's move to the bar. I want to check to see how many of them are here,' she said into his ear.

Squeezing her hand in agreement, Zej led Keix through the dance floor again. Moving along the walls was not the best idea since people tended to watch and analyse others around them when they were not losing themselves in the heavy hitting music. Like before, Keix and Zej pretended to dance as they squeezed past couples who were glued together from their faces to their toes while sidestepping individuals showing off their dancing skills. Keix had a hard time deciding whether the partiers around these dancers were admiring or avoiding the energetic moves.

As they neared the bar, the music track switched to one with a more sedate beat and the spinning lights slowed to match it. Still swaying to the music, Keix scanned the mass of bodies. Her heart skipped a beat when she saw a pair of glowing eyes in the crowd. She pulled Zej into an embrace and whispered in his ear. 'Seyfer's here.' At the words, she felt him tense up although he didn't pull away.

'Are you sure?'

'Don't look. He might not have seen us yet.' Keix prayed that her words were true as she clung on to Zej for cover.

A buzz from Keix's pocket told her Pod had texted again. She fumbled with the phone.

How's the situation? Shall we proceed?

Seyfer's here. RUN!

R u sure?

Keix almost screamed in exasperation. *YES! Go now! Zej and I will find a way to meet you at the safe house*, she typed.

She jammed the phone into the back pocket of her jeans and peeked past Zej's shoulders. An icy hand closed around her heart when her worst suspicions were confirmed. Even at this distance, without catching his eye, there was no mistaking Seyfer's height and the cocky way he carried himself. Keix could picture the insanity lurking behind those amber eyes. She shuddered. He wouldn't be alone.

Panic overtook Keix as she turned on her heel. It was unlikely that Seyfer had identified her in this crowd, but she wasn't going to take any chances. She tugged Zej towards the back exit, in the opposite direction from Seyfer. Along the way, she cast surreptitious glances around them, identifying four more partygoers who were behaving stiffly. She couldn't tell if it was the spinning lights or her anxiety that was making her sick. Pushing through the crowd with Zej, they tried hard not to draw attention to themselves. She almost cried with relief when they exited the building without a hitch. Taking in a deep breath of the cool night air to calm her nerves, she scanned the area. The back exit of the club led out to a deserted alleyway. Streetlights from the main road spilled over the low buildings, casting long shadows everywhere. Pulling out the phone, she typed to Pod. *Where are you guys? We're out of the club.*

'We shouldn't go back to the hovercar in case we have a tail,' said Zej, looking around.

Keix nodded. 'I told Pod that we'd meet them back at the safe house.' She looked at the phone. Pod hadn't replied yet.

Going to make sure we're not tailed before we head back. Text back to let us know you guys are fine.

The lack of response from Pod was worrying her.

'Let's get out of here first.' Keix made to move but a voice stopped her in her tracks.

'And where do you think you're going?'

Dread flooded her. She could recognize that voice anywhere.

Seven figures appeared from the shadows and blocked their way. Seyfer was standing in the middle.

Keix heard Zej's sharp intake of breath as the leader of the group strolled towards them.

'We meet again, Kulcan,' he said. 'And I see you've brought your friend too. It's a pleasure—' he made a small little bow not unlike the one he had given Keix before, '—Zej.'

'What do you want with us, Seyfer?' Keix was asking the obvious, but she thought that the longer she stalled, the more likely it was that Dace, Pod and Maii were going to get away. Her eyes darted round, wondering if there was any way for them to escape.

Seyfer gave a dismissive wave of his hand. 'What can I possibly want except for you to join us, Keix?'

'Stay away from her.' Zej's voice was low and dangerous as he stepped in front of Keix.

'Oh, don't take this the wrong way, Zej,' said Seyfer with a grating laugh, 'but I doubt your epic love will endure Keix's transition.'

Keix fought down a shiver. Before she could answer, another familiar voice pierced the air.

'Let us go, you maniac!' It was Pod.

Atros soldiers flanked him and Dace. Both of them were trying to break out of their captors' grips. Keix's heart dropped as she saw Maii slumped unconscious between two soldiers. Zej had said that the sedative that they had used on Rold was fatal to those with Ifarl blood. She prayed they hadn't used the same drug on Maii.

'So glad that you could join us, Pod. Dace.' Seyfer's delight was evident. 'Sorry we had to knock Maii out. Can't have her powers interfere with our grand plan.'

'I'm going to kill you!' Pod was putting up an admirable fight against his guards. But his threats only seemed to amuse Seyfer.

'Well, I just wanted to be here for our little reunion before we moved you guys somewhere more comfortable,' he said and waved his hand.

At his signal, the soldiers pulled out their guns and started firing at Keix and Zej.

Almost immediately, Keix felt a prick at her neck. She knew it was a sedative before she even felt its effects. Zej dropped to the ground beside her as the drug made its way through his body. Pod and Dace slumped forward too. Reaching into the power at the back of her mind, Keix channelled a dose of it through her body to burn away the tranquillizer. She pretended to fall as the grogginess faded, moving into position to launch herself at Seyfer. A figure with glowing eyes like Seyfer jumped out before Keix could reach Seyfer. The face she saw made her gasp.

No, it couldn't be . . .

A blunt object struck the back of Keix's head, halting her train of thoughts. She only managed to utter one word before darkness overtook her. 'Vin?'

Keix awoke with a start. Bright white light flooded the room she was in. It took a while for her eyes to adjust to the brightness. When her vision cleared, she saw that the space had a high ceiling and was bigger than the ones she had occupied at the hut and plant. She was alone, sitting up on a clinical bed pushed against the wall; on the other side stood a toilet and small basin. Keix stood up and walked towards the opposite wall of vertical bars. Her breaths turned into little wisps of cloud when it met the sterile, frosty air, devoid of any characteristics, drifting in through the poles. Her head was throbbing and there was a faint ringing in her ears, which she assumed was due to both the loud music at the party and the blow to her skull. She couldn't determine which Atros facility she was in. The cell she was in was on one side of a hexagonal space. In the cell directly opposite hers, a figure was sprawled on the bed.

'Pod?' she called out in a whisper. The word scraped at her throat. The person didn't move, but she heard a low shuffling sound as she swallowed and tried again, this time louder. 'Zej? Dace? Maii?'

'You're up.' Maii's voice came from the room to her right.

Keix turned her head to see Maii stepping into view. Sighing with relief, she said, 'You're okay. I thought the sedative that they used was fatal to those with Ifarl blood.'

Maii shrugged. 'They must have changed the drug. Either the new formula doesn't work very well, or they used too small a dose. I woke up just as they were moving us here. I tried to command them to let me out, but I guess my compulsion doesn't work against those yellow-eyed freaks. Although, I did manage to clock one in the nose. Thought I heard a crack,' she added with a smug smile.

'I don't think it works on me anymore either,' Keix admitted.

'What doesn't work on you? The compulsion?'

Keix nodded.

'Really? Laugh like a maniac,' Maii commanded.

The power of Maii's charm dissolved when it reached Keix's mind. She frowned at her in response. 'What kind of test was that?'

'Hmm,' Maii pondered. 'A mildly entertaining one, I hoped, if it had worked.'

'Keix? Maii?' Zej's face appeared between the bars of another cell. 'Where are we?'

'An Atros facility, I believe,' replied Keix.

'Boy, I hope we're in PEER.' Pod's voice was hoarse, probably from all the shouting that he had done earlier. 'That would mean things are still going according to plan.'

Maii's laugh sounded like a melodious jingle.

'You and I have a very different understanding of the phrase "going according to plan",' Dace cut in.

'Do you remember seeing anything like this in the blueprint of PEER, Pod?' asked Zej.

Pod deliberated for a couple of second. 'Yes, I think so. But this could be a common structure in other Atros facilities too.'

'Is there a way out of here?' interrupted Keix, looking around. The entire pentagon seemed to be hermetically sealed. Even if they managed to get out of their cells, she couldn't see any way out of this place. She walked to the corner of her prison and grasped two adjacent bars. Reaching into the energy at the back of her head, she channelled a steady stream of power to her hands as she tried to bend the poles, her brows furrowing at the strain.

'You're trying to bend the metal poles,' stated Dace with a mix of amusement and incredulity.

Keix's body grew warm from the strain, but the bars refused to budge.

Maii faked a yawn. 'Let me know how that works out for you.'

Letting out a frustrated sigh, Keix said, 'Well, at least I tried.' She leaned her back against the poles and slid down into a sitting position. How long would they be stuck here? What was Atros planning to do with them? More importantly, was there any way of fixing Vin? The image of her best friend with crazy eyes like Seyfer's sent chills down her spine.

Keix lulled herself into a meditative state as the mood in the prison turned grimmer and each of them turned their thoughts and frustration inwards. Occasionally, Keix would hear a long-drawn sigh or the rhythmic thudding of someone's boots against the concrete floor as they paced around in their jail cell. But no one spoke—not even Pod.

A mechanical whirr brought everyone to their feet. They rushed to the bars and watched as a circle descended from the centre of the ceiling. Three pairs of Atros-issued boots came into sight.

Goosebumps dotted Keix's skin but it had nothing to do with the freezing temperature in the cell. She held her breath like she was anticipating the unveiling of some secret. When she finally saw the faces of the people who had come to visit, she choked up.

No, she wasn't shocked to see Seyfer in the group. Nor was she surprised to see Vin, all cleaned up—with her pink hair chopped to her shoulders and still skinny—with her glowing eyes. It was the man standing in the middle that crushed the last shred of Keix's fighting spirit and any hope she held out about leaving this place with her friends. He didn't have his trademark cape, but neither did he have the yellow eyes of his comrades—they were still as grey, still as keen.

With much difficulty, Keix forced his name out of her lips. 'Oron.'

13

Imprisoned

'Oron?' Pod and Zej echoed Keix, confusion apparent in their voices. Since their mentor had come down the platform facing her, the two boys had had no idea that Oron was among their captors until she had said his name.

'You know him?' asked Dace. 'What the hell is going on?'

Maii was, once again, characteristically quiet.

Neither Seyfer nor Vin showed any sign of joining in this exchange. Vin was staring into thin air with a look of extreme boredom on her face. Seyfer, however, was smirking at Keix with an air of superiority. She avoided his eyes and focused her attention on Oron instead.

'Keix. Pod. And Zej,' said Oron, turning around.

Pod stared at Oron with bulging eyes and Zej staggered backwards, shaking his head in denial.

Nothing in Oron's bearing seemed to have changed— his voice was still deep and booming when he said, 'It is great to see you all. Even though I'm sorry that it had to come to this.' His eyes were piercing and intense, just as Keix remembered them.

'Atros said you were dead,' shouted Pod, having found his voice.

Zej's whisper was a huge contrast to his friend's. 'Why would you do this?'

Keix thought she saw a hint of sorrow in Oron's eyes as he turned back to look at her. 'I don't owe any of you an explanation, but I will give it anyway.' He paced the pentagon like he was giving one of his usual briefings. 'Atros put out the news of my demise because I was reassigned to head a secret department called the Acquisitions team. As all of you may know, paranormal activity has been on the increase. There is no such thing as sending those spectres into a black hole—our technology isn't that advanced. And since these ghosts can't die again, we were running out of places to hold them. We needed to find a way to fight or control them in order to protect our citizens. After much experimentation, we found out that not only could we control the spirits if we bound their energy to living beings, but that the process endowed these people with enhanced speed and strength. It's a win-win situation for Atros.'

A sick feeling rose from the pit of Keix's stomach at Oron's matter-of-fact explanation. She would never have thought that the mentor that she had liked and respected so much would be so blind to the downsides of this so-called way of 'protecting citizens'. She couldn't keep her anger in check any longer. 'But can't you see that these hybrids are monsters? Or does Atros even care, since you're so chummy with Odats too?' she cried.

Vin turned to look at Keix with a raised eyebrow at her outburst. 'Tsk, Keix. I'm hurt. I thought we were best friends,' she said without a hint of warmth.

Seyfer's smirk stayed firmly in place. 'Well, I'm sure that will change once she transitions. Or, she could dump you for me. I think we've developed a certain affinity for each other, haven't we, Keix?'

There was that word again. Transition. It sounded even more sinister coming out of his mouth.

'You can have her then. I think I like my Ifarls better,' said Vin, giving Maii a wide smile.

'Stay away from her!' Pod, Zej and Dace said at the same time.

'Looks like we have some tough competition, Seyfer,' Vin laughed.

Keix couldn't suppress a shudder. While her friend's laughter used to be genuine and contagious, it just sounded indifferent and cold now.

'Enough,' Oron chided his officers. 'Anyway, we just came down to make sure that all of you are in the proper condition to be transitioned. Keix, you will be the first since you've been prepped for it. I hope that the rest of you will soon be able to transition too. It will be your honour to serve the citizens of Atros.'

'What a load of crap,' mumbled Maii.

'You took the words right out of my mouth, Maii,' said Pod.

Keix wanted to laugh at their synergy. Maii's complete lack of fear at the threat of impending torture was pretty impressive. *Or maybe she just puts on a really good game face*, she thought.

Oron seemed unperturbed by their reactions. He retrieved a small device from his pocket and pushed the toggle. The circle floated back up to the ceiling, carrying with it three of the craziest people Keix hoped she would never see ever again.

Silence engulfed the space once more. Everyone had been rendered speechless by Oron's visit. They had already come to the conclusion that there was no way out of the cells. And even if they escaped from this prison, how would they ever make it out of the sector?

The robotic whirr sounded again, jolting all of them out of their despondent thoughts. This time around, only one person came down the platform. He was pushing a trolley with containers on it and the blue of his curly hair clashed with his uniform.

Keix had to clasp her hand over her mouth to prevent herself from calling out his name—it was J. She searched his eyes for a yellow glow, the tell-tale sign of a hybrid, and let out a relieved sigh when she saw that he hadn't been 'transitioned', to use Oron's term. She looked over at Zej and saw the rekindling of hope in his eyes.

'I don't really understand why I'm doing this, but I've been ordered to deliver food to you guys,' he said by way of greeting. Turning to Keix first, he passed her a box from the trolley.

As Keix reached out to collect the container, J pressed a piece of paper into her hands. 'Camera?' Keix mouthed.

J shook his head, then turned to Maii's cell.

'Let us out. Right now,' Maii commanded as Keix glanced down at the note. It was typewritten and there was no signature on it.

Seyfer will visit you in five minutes' time. The bars will open then. It is your best chance to escape. J will lead you out.

'I can't,' J answered Maii. 'I don't have the key.'

Maii uttered her second order before Keix could stop her. 'Then get out of here now and find someone who can.'

'Maii, wait!' Keix hissed. 'He's on our side!'

Maii looked surprised but she retracted her compulsion just as J was heading back to the platform.

'What the hell was that for?' J threw her an offended glare. He ran his hands over his scalp as if the action could dissipate the strange sensation of being subjected to an Ifarl's orders. 'Like K said, I'm on your side.'

'And I was supposed to know that, how?' Maii's voice was dripping with sarcasm.

'So I'm assuming there's no surveillance down here,' said Keix, trying to defuse the tension.

J shook his head in affirmation. 'I don't think so.'

'Then why did you behave like you had no idea who we are?' Pod jumped in.

'Well, you can never be too careful,' J was still indignant.

'There's no time for this,' interjected Zej. He turned to J, 'Can you get us out of here?'

Keix answered on J's behalf. 'J handed me this note. It says that Seyfer will be down here in a few minutes. The bars to our cell will open then. All we have to do is to knock him out and J will lead us out. Right, J? J's with Oka, by the way.'

'Oh, so you're J,' said Dace, comprehension dawning in his face. 'Dace here, by the way. We've spoken before.'

J nodded. 'I need to go back upstairs to avoid awkward questions. Once you head up, exit the holding room. I'll be waiting right outside the door.'

'Hold up! Are we in PEER?' asked Pod. At J's nod, his face lit up. 'Which cell are we in?'

'H6-K. It's in—'

'Area I!' Pod couldn't keep the excitement and glee out of his voice.

Keix could see the wheels turning inside his head. And sure enough, after a couple of seconds, he added, 'We're just six levels below the main control room.'

'Which means we have a shot at getting the others out too,' added Maii, deducing his train of thought.

J looked a little bewildered, but he hurried back on to the platform and disappeared from view before Keix could ask about the origin of the note.

Adrenalin pumped through Keix as she realized they had a fighting chance now.

'Well, five of us against a crazy guy who has enhanced strength and speed because he's bonded with some paranormal voodoo,' summed up Dace. 'Should be a breeze.'

The bars slid open from the bottom right on schedule, coinciding with the circular platform moving downwards.

Keix and the rest had lain on their backs, ready to roll out of their cells instead of waiting for the bars to rise up all the way. Seyfer's boots came within Dace's reach and, with the element of surprise on his side, Dace succeeded in grabbing Seyfer's ankles and pulling them towards him. The hybrid let out a grunt as his back hit the rim of the platform. But his recovery was almost immediate. He let loose a kick at his assailant and a crunch sounded as his boot connected with Dace's nose.

Pod and Zej leapt to restrain each of Seyfer's legs.

The circular platform was now waist high.

Blood was streaming from Dace's nose, but that didn't stop him from pouncing on Seyfer. He and Maii grabbed on to the hybrid's arms and held him down at the shoulders. Keix jumped on Seyfer's chest and threw a punch at his temple—but the move did little more than draw a laugh from him. In a show of power, he threw all of them off and stood up. Keix and the rest staggered backwards.

Anger seized Keix. She reached into herself for her power and leapt at Seyfer again. With uncanny precision, he sidestepped her move. Because of the strength that she put into the jump, she hit her shoulder against one of the barred walls.

Pod, Zej, Dace and Maii circled Seyfer as Keix got to her feet. Even though his attention was focused on Keix, it was difficult to find an opening to attack.

Seyfer gave her a malicious smile and stepped towards her. Taking advantage of the change in his stance, Pod and Zej lunged at him. Even with their combined weight, Seyfer managed to stay on his feet.

Even with blood pouring from his nose, Dace leapt at Seyfer from behind, hooking an arm around his neck and squeezing. The strain caused the shade of Dace's face to match his dripping gore, but he clung on with resolution.

Instead of trying to loosen the chokehold, Seyfer threw out his arms at Pod and Zej. The force pushed both of them backwards and they crumpled against the bars, groaning in pain. Maii charged at Seyfer. She kicked his waist and followed through with a strike to the back of his knee. This time, the momentum and the accuracy of the hits at these vulnerable spots made him stagger forward.

Keix channelled a burst of energy and kicked out at Seyfer's head. The tip of her boot hit his temple with a sickening crack. His head whipped to the side. The move flung Dace off, who joined Pod and Zej on the floor.

With a roar, Seyfer swung his fists at the person nearest to him—Maii. A single hit sent her flying backwards towards the bars.

'SEYFER, STOP!' Maii called out. Her voice was steady and authoritative even though she struggled to stand.

The force in the command made the hair at the back of Keix's neck stand. From the ringing vibration in the air, she could tell that Maii had directed all her mind-control powers into this command.

Seyfer came to a halt and turned his attention away from Keix. A mirthless laugh emitted from his open mouth. 'You think to command me, *Ifar?*' he asked Maii. 'ME? A hybrid imbued with the powers of the supernatural? I am invincible!' He tilted his head back and cackled again.

That dramatic reaction proved to be his downfall.

Keix raced forward and aimed all the glowing energy she could gather into her punch. When her fist connected with Seyfer's chest, she felt red-hot heat exploding out from the impact. It was like a raging fire had burst in her hand. She cried out in pain. It took all her willpower to resist the instinct to snatch her hand back. Somehow, she was aware that she had to maintain contact in order for the power that she brought forward to work. The heat spread to the rest of her body, engulfing her to the point where she couldn't breathe.

In an instant, the flames faded. A rush of icy-cold sensation that grew with vehemence took the place of the scorching heat. Driven delirious by the abrupt change, Keix had the bizarre image of herself bursting into fire and her friends hurrying forward to douse her in ice water before shoving her into a mammoth-sized freezer. All she could see now was white. There was no presence of any other colour in her vision. Then it became dark. Not a trace of the brightness from before was left behind. It was a black so intense it threatened to swallow her up. *Is this what a real black hole looks like?* Keix wondered.

Something made Keix sway. The movement melted the darkness away. Stars appeared. Someone was calling her name repeatedly. *No*, she corrected herself, *there were several someones.* The voices differed in pitch and emotion.

Keix swayed harder. With each movement, awareness returned. Her eyes flew open to see four concerned faces looking down on her.

'Thank goodness,' exclaimed Pod. 'We thought you were dead.'

'*Pod* thought you were dead. I told him I could still feel a pulse,' Dace interjected.

'How are you feeling?' Zej asked.

Even Maii spoke. 'I told you to pace yourself.'

Keix sat up. Her body screamed in protest at the sudden movement. 'What happened?' she asked. She looked around and saw Seyfer lying spreadeagled on the floor in front of her.

'Well, you punched him,' answered Dace, gesturing to Seyfer. 'Then you sort of glowed.'

'Before you fell back,' quipped Maii.

Everything came back to Keix in a flash. 'Is he dead?'

A round of shrugs followed her query.

'He didn't seem to have a pulse the last time we checked,' said Zej.

'But he's not glowing—like normal people do when they die—so we aren't sure,' supplied Pod.

Moving towards Seyfer's body, Keix said, 'We have to get out of here.'

Without protest, everyone clambered onto the platform. Dace and Zej insisted on standing on either side of Keix, holding her arms in a firm grip. She tried to will the exhaustion away and prayed that her muscles, which still felt raw and abused, would hold up. Reaching for the well of energy in her mind, she heaved a sigh of relief to find that it was steadily replenishing itself.

When the platform reached its apex, the five of them stepped out and moved towards the only door in the room. Pod opened it to find J standing guard outside as planned.

'What took you so long?' asked J. His gaze landed on Dace's bloodied nose, so he added, 'It was five against one!'

Dace gave an offended grunt.

'You didn't hear the commotion?' asked Pod in disbelief.

'The room's soundproofed.'

'Enough with the small talk,' interrupted Maii. 'We need to get the others and out of here now.'

'Others?' J's uncertainty was written all over his face.

At that moment, a shrill ringing filled the air. The six of them stopped in their tracks and exchanged astonished looks at the sound of the alarm. It was clear what was on everyone's mind, and Pod's exasperated outburst pretty much summed it up, 'No . . . Not Odats again!'

'The main control room's to the right,' shouted Pod over the din. He gestured to the fork at the end of the hallway.

The six of them tore down the corridor. The place would be crawling with Atros soldiers and Odats soon.

Sure enough, a group of soldiers rushed at them as they approached the T-junction.

'Go! We'll hold them off,' cried Maii.

Keix nodded. The situation was too volatile for her to protest.

'Pod, come on!' pressed Keix. He had to go with her because he was the only one who could hack into the system.

With great reluctance, Pod tore his eyes from Maii and said, 'We're going to need an authorization pass.'

'J, you're coming too,' said Keix.

J looked half scared, half excited at this change of plans. But he followed right behind Pod and Keix.

Just as Pod had claimed, the control room was up six levels and a short distance from their cell. To their surprise, they encountered no resistance on their way there. The stairs were empty despite the alarm. The Atros people they dashed past were in white coats, like the one Keix had worn during her escape from PEER. While their faces registered shock and confusion at Keix and Pod's out-of-place leather outfits, J's uniform seemed to reassure them that there was nothing alarming about this strange trio.

J's pass got them into the control room and Keix dispatched the two puzzled guards with lightning speed.

Pod's fingers flew across the control board and within seconds, the alarms were blaring even more loudly than Keix thought was possible.

'I've just set off the alarms in the whole facility, even the public areas. This should buy us some time. Do you still have your tracker with you?'

Keix nodded. Seyfer and his subordinates hadn't thought to search them since they had managed to bring the group in together.

'Okay. Take J in case you run into any closed doors that I can't open in time.' Pod fished around one of the unconscious guard's pockets. He retrieved a mini radio and tossed it to Keix.

'I'll guide you from here.'

When Keix hesitated, Pod gave her a push. 'Go on,' he said. 'I'll be fine. I'll lock myself in here.'

'What if they wake up?' Keix's tone was filled with worry.

'Well, you could—'

J had taken out a gun and shot at the unconscious bodies before Pod could finish his sentence. 'There, they'll be sedated for—' J looked at his watch '—at least the next hour.'

'—do that.' Pod looked both amused and impressed.

Once J and Keix got out of the control room, they ran into three Atros soldiers. Like those in white coats, the troopers' first response to the odd couple was confusion. Their momentary hesitation was enough for J and Keix to knock them out.

The underground cave was much farther from the control room than Keix had expected. Between the running and fighting off of random units of Atros soldiers, the strain was starting to get to her. This time, however, she heeded Maii's advice to pace herself, drawing on the power in sparse amounts, and only when absolutely necessary. The rush of adrenalin helped keep her on her toes too.

'I'll need clothes. And hoverboards. As many as you can find,' said Keix between heavy breaths when Pod indicated that they were nearing the underground cave.

'Supply closet,' gestured J to a half-opened door.

Keix knew they had lucked out when she found two old hoverboards and a shelf full of white coats in the room.

A surreal feeling overcame her when she stepped into the dark cavern. She recalled the last time she stood in this exact spot and shuddered to think about what would have happened if Zej had never joined Oka. Would she still be trapped in here like the rest of the people she was going to bust out?

'Okay, get ready to receive your alien babies,' said Pod over the radio.

And right on cue, black wired cocoons began bursting through the water's surface and delivering naked bodies to her. There were at least a dozen of them, many of whom looked less frail than Keix when she had been rescued by Zej. Some were even capable of speech despite their weakened condition. Keix deduced that they had to have been here for a much shorter time, which was why their bodies weren't as feeble as hers had been.

'Are we done here?' Keix asked Pod.

'Yes, just one more.'

J helped usher the survivors out in pairs as they made their way up the tunnel.

Keix clenched her fists as the last cocoon made its way to her. When she saw the person's face, she couldn't conceal her astonishment.

'Lyndon?'

From the looks of his skeletal frame, Keix gathered that Lyndon must have been imprisoned longer than the rest of them. It figured, since he had been caught in the black hole around the same time as Keix was captured. He could barely stand on his own, much less answer her. She flung a coat over his body and with some difficulty, helped him up the hoverboard out of the underground prison.

'Hey, Lyndon. Hold on to me, okay? We need to keep the hoverboard steady on the ride up,' urged Keix. She let out the breath she was holding when Lyndon gave a small nod in reply.

A bigger surprise was waiting for Keix when they got out of the vertical tunnel. Machillian was standing there with the orange-haired girl she had met at the plant. The Oka leader nodded in acknowledgement when he saw her. Keix picked up her jaw. These two were the last people she thought she would run into here, considering Oka's aversion to 'acting without concrete evidence'.

Yet here they were, looking like they had just emerged from a fight. Machillian sported a half-clotted cut above his right eyebrow while a bruise was forming on the girl's left cheek.

'Lola and I will get them out of here,' said Machillian in that raspy voice of his. 'There's a group of us here to help.'

'I called for backup,' explained J at Keix's incredulous look.

Pod's urgent voice broke the awkward tension. 'Keix! You've got to get back here. Quick. Maii and the rest are being overrun by Atros soldiers.'

14

Dead End

Keix rounded a corner just in time to see a wave of soldiers surging at her friends. She and J had picked up Pod from the control room before rushing to Maii, Dace and Zej's location. A quick count told Keix that they were outnumbered—six of them to at least fifty-odd Atros soldiers. And the pattering of boots that was getting louder seemed to indicate that more troopers were on the way. All of them were dressed in standard Atros uniforms like J, but they had their helmets on, the tinted visors obscuring their faces. Keix could only hope that they weren't hybrids like Seyfer. *If I had to expend so much energy just to take down one of them, what were the chances of us getting out of here with all these people charging at us?*

'They're coming from both ends!' shouted Maii.

Keix snapped out of her ugly reflections. Soldiers had cut off their chance of a retreat along the doorless hallway. Their enemies had doubled in number. Even though it was clear that the troopers had the upper hand here, they were approaching Keix's group with caution.

J's cover was blown since he didn't have his helmet on—that and the fact that he was running with them instead of against. Without a word, they formed two rows, back to back. Zej and Dace stood to Keix's side. J, Pod and Maii formed another wall, facing the advancing troopers. J and Dace were the only ones with weapons. J was brandishing a baton while Dace had a tranquilizer gun in his hand. Keix realized J must have passed the weapon to Dace because he was the only one who looked to be injured; clotted blood surrounded his nose, which was likely broken.

The tension in the hallway stretched tauter and tauter with each passing second as the alarms persisted. Then it snapped at the same time as the shrill ringing was abruptly cut off. Silence whooshed into the space, as if signalling for the fight to commence. The sea of brown and green rushed at the thin line of black from both sides, like waves crashing on breakwater.

Dace fired at the soldiers approaching him. But the darts ricocheted off their protective gear.

Zej charged at his nearest enemy. He grabbed the trooper's wrist and twisted it upwards, then dug an elbow into his chest. With the temporary edge he gained, he yanked off the helmet then shouted, 'Dace, now!'

Comprehending Zej's intention in a split second, Dace shot the guard he was holding down at close range. The dart pierced their opponent's neck. As the sedative took effect, he stumbled forward and Zej loosened his hold.

Another trooper came at Dace with a tranquilizer gun of his own. With lightning speed, Dace evaded the dart. His back curved into a crouch and he executed a kick at his enemy's ankle. The soldier fell to the ground from the pain and Dace flipped up his visor and fired a dart right between his clear green eyes.

With his immediate opponent down, Dace continued firing at the troopers that Zej was shoving his way. Once he had emptied his cartridge, Dace threw the gun to the side and picked up another one from one of the bodies at his feet—a small pile was starting to form there, now that he and Zej had developed an effective system of dispatching their opponents.

Wielding a baton that she had taken from the first soldier that she knocked out with her bare hands, Keix struck down five more troopers with ease. Like the rest, she had a system. The first step was punching those who were closing in on her—stomach, groin or chest, it didn't matter. Then, as they staggered from the impact, she would wrench their helmets off before delivering a blow to their temple to render them unconscious. With a little help from the well of power, Keix was having next-to-zero trouble overpowering her opponents. Still, the slight ache in her muscles served as a constant reminder for her to not overstretch herself as she dodged the tranquilizer darts being fired in her direction.

The pile of unconscious bodies that Zej and Dace had created shielded them from the drugged darts too. Only one trooper could get to Zej at any one time, making the attack less chaotic compared to before.

Keix turned around to check on the progress of the rest of the group. She did a double take when she saw a helmeted figure fighting alongside Maii. Pod must have donned the headgear to protect himself against the darts. The outfits that Maii had picked out for them were as hardy as they were stylish, as Keix found out herself when she saw several tranquilizer darts stuck on the thick leather of her jacket.

The pile of bodies on Pod's side was more scattered as he and Maii were taking down their opponents individually. Keix's heart dropped when she couldn't spot J. Was he among one of the unconscious troopers? But the question was answered a split second after it formed. Her sharp vision caught one green and brown soldier surreptitiously tripping the others as he wended his way through them.

Pride and hope surged in Keix as she saw that the soldiers' numbers were dwindling. The majority of the soldiers in their midst were sprawled on the floor. Less than two handfuls of them were still standing. A part of her was secretly appalled at the soldiers' poor showing. Hand-to-hand combat was an integral part of ATI training, after all.

'This way,' called out J, pointing down the hallway.

The rest of them followed, defeating the last eight of the Atros troopers with practised ease. Not a groan or moan was heard as Keix and her comrades remained the only ones standing. They looked at each other, their chests heaving.

Taking care to not stumble over the mass of tangled limbs and torsos, Keix urged the group forward as she brought up the rear.

Moments later, despite navigating two stretches of corridors without meeting any more soldiers, an uneasy feeling started gnawing at Keix.

A stench of decaying food pervaded the air at the same moment.

'Odats,' snarled Maii to the surprise of everyone else except Keix.

Pod stopped in his tracks. 'What?'

'Odats are catching up with us,' confirmed Keix. Dace and J, who were at the head of the line, tensed.

'How many of them are there?' asked Dace, turning to J.

'I have no idea.' J's expression was solemn. 'But we have to split up. There's no way we can take them head-on.'

Pod's nostrils flared at J's suggestion. 'No way we're splitting up again. How do you know we can't take them down?'

'Yeah, we just mowed through more than a hundred Atros soldiers,' agreed Dace, pulling out two tranquilizer guns.

'Have you actually *fought* any Odats before?' J asked in a derisive tone.

'Keix took down more than a dozen by herself at the plant,' said Zej with a groan before staggering forward. Dace and Pod rushed forward to break his fall just in time. When Dace brushed the side of Zej's torso with his arm, he grimaced. They pulled up his top to reveal a purpling bruise at the bottom of his ribcage. Keix thought it was remarkable how Zej had managed to keep up with the rest of them given the beating that he had taken.

'I'm fine,' said Zej through gritted teeth. He tried to straighten up, but it was obvious that the pain was taking a toll on him.

'We have to get you out of here first,' said Keix to Zej. 'You're in no condition to go up against Odats.' She added to the rest, 'I'll hold them off while you guys escape.'

'I'll stay with you,' Maii said. Her tone signalled that there was no room for negotiation.

'Me too,' declared Pod.

J nodded. 'Dace and I will get Zej to Machillian and gang. This whole facility is underground and there are only three ways out of this area—one elevator and two emergency stairs,' he said, gesturing in opposite directions.

'Don't worry,' said Pod. 'I have the blueprints of this place memorized. You guys go ahead. I'll take care of the girls.'

'Right. We'll see you outside,' urged Keix.

The foul smell was growing so strong that Pod was scrunching up his face. Dace and J set off with Zej, who looked to be on the verge of fainting, between them.

Keix, Maii and Pod looked at each other and ran in the opposite direction. Hoping that Zej and the rest wouldn't run into any more enemy troops, Keix turned her attention to the unit of monsters headed her way.

Once again, déjà vu struck her—except this time, it was manifold. The eerie wave-like movement that she encountered in PEER had manifested into a torrent. By the dozens, mustard heads suspended in the air floated towards the three of them. Their Atros uniforms, the exact same shade of white as their surroundings, failed to disguise the vileness of the creatures wearing them.

Keix looked around for a more strategic location from which to fight their opponents as they neared. She had barely utilized her power when fighting the troopers just now. But even with the energy blazing within her, she wasn't confident that the three of them could take down all of these Odats without significantly depleting her strength.

In spite of the looming danger, Pod seemed unperturbed. In all seriousness, he asked, 'Do you know that they don't wear helmets because even they themselves can't stand their own bad breath?'

Keix's look of exasperation turned into one of amusement when Maii gave one of her musical laughs at Pod's outrageous comment.

As the first two Odats rushed at them, Keix was fervently grateful that this part of PEER had narrow corridors. With the beasts' broad stature, only two of them could approach her party at a time. She hoped that this bottleneck would work to their favour.

A sharp hiss filled the air as Pod fired the sedative gun at one of them. Pod's aim was true, but he had underestimated the hardiness of their enemies' lumpy skin; the needle bounced off the hide and fell to the floor with a soft clatter.

Pod cursed. Eyes narrowed in concentration and all humour gone, he continued training his pistol at his target. Keix readied the baton she had held on to from her recent fight and was glad to see that Maii was gripping two of her own. As the monsters leading the attack came within arm's reach of Keix, two more shots sounded. If Keix hadn't noticed the tiny dart protruding from the eyes of the monsters, she might have been shocked to see them collapsing at her feet. Like puppets with their strings cut, there was no change in the black pit that formed their irises as Keix's group stepped backwards to see a repeat of this stop-and-drop scene.

Keix glanced to her side to see that she wasn't the only one impressed with Pod's sharpshooting skills. Maii had on her face an expression of admiration as she tossed one of her batons to Pod, who had emptied his cartridge on seven more guards. The small mound of bodies did little to staunch the pace of the Odats as they trampled over their colleagues with little more than a grunt. Together, Maii and Pod faced one of their foes while Keix engaged the one beside it.

The Odat facing Keix looked to be twice her size. It brought its white-gloved hand, clenched into a fist, down with remarkable speed on her head. Keix ducked with a swiftness to match and directed a trickle of her power into her raised arm to deflect the blow. A dull pain reverberated from the point of contact down to the tip of her toes, making her wince. She was quite sure that her bone would have cracked if she hadn't reinforced it with her power. But before she could recover, her opponent sent out another punch which caught her on the cheek and sent her tumbling backwards.

'Keix!' Maii and Pod both shouted at the same time.

'I'm fine,' replied Keix, barely getting the words out of her hurting jaws. She reached for more energy and sprang to her feet as soon as her back touched the floor. Seeing her friends' adversary advance on them when they were momentarily distracted, she warned, 'Look out!'

Maii and Pod reacted with uncanny rapport. Seizing their enemy's arm on each side, they pulled it forward. The sudden force made it stumble and they took the chance to deliver hits to its temples with the bases of their batons. With a grunt, the guard fell on its face. For good measure, Maii gave its nape another thump and a crack sounded, but it remained stretched out on the floor.

With no time to celebrate their little victory, Maii and Pod turned to their next challenger. Keix's own opponent swung out another arm at her. She ducked again and sent an unhesitating kick at its head, which snapped back with the force of the blow. Another Odat took the place of its fallen comrade and rushed towards her with both its arms out. She continued dodging and returning well-aimed hits, taking down the same number of enemies as Maii and Pod combined.

Two by two, the creatures went down. But the rate at which they were advancing on them made it difficult to switch to an offensive play from their current defensive stance. Unlike the Atros soldiers who were trained and had a set method to their attacks, these brutes were unpredictable.

Keix's party had backed up so much that they were almost at the T-junction they had come from. If they moved just a few more steps, they would lose the advantage that the narrow hallway provided them with.

Glancing over the shoulder of her current foe, which looked no different from the Odat she had just knocked down, Keix tried to estimate the number of Odats that were still pressing in on them. But all she could see was a blur of white and brownish-yellow, like someone trying to swirl mud into white paint.

'Can we—' Maii paused to evade a heavy gloved fist, '—make a run for it?' Between laboured breaths, she slammed her weapon into the face of the oncoming Odat. Beside her, Pod's face was red with exertion. Sweat poured down his forehead as he struggled to keep up with the never-ending onslaught of monsters.

Keix was feeling the strain too. Once again, the precision of her attacks was diminishing. She was just about to reply when a shout came from their left side. It was Dace. 'Over here!' he shouted. His head and shoulders were jutting out from a section of the wall. Whether it was another corridor or room, Keix couldn't tell.

'Pod! Maii! Go! I'll buy you some time,' Keix said as she fended off another Odat with a spinning kick.

'What? No, we'll go to—' A loud crack sounded as a guard clocked Pod in the head, cutting off his protest. Without missing a beat, Maii grabbed hold of Pod before he fell to the ground. She tossed his weapon to Keix, who caught it with her free hand as she sidestepped an incoming punch from her opponent. Keix could have sworn she heard Maii mutter 'idiot', before she nodded in response to Keix's suggestion and readied herself to run, supporting an unconscious Pod with one arm while battling another foe with her free arm.

Keix tapped into more of the power, concentrating on enhancing her speed and agility. This was no time for measured blows. She had to create some breathing room for her comrades to get to Dace. She glanced back to make sure that Maii and Pod had a good headstart, then she turned to face the line of monsters closing in on her. Three of them were rushing at her like the head of an arrow— the rest following closely behind. If not for the lack of order and grace of these creatures, this would have been an impossible mob to defeat.

Keix waited until the first Odat was within reach, then she directed a kick at its jaw. There was a sickening crunch as the beast's head snapped upwards before falling backwards onto its fellow soldiers. In the split second that the two other Odats behind it took to shove it away, Keix launched herself at the one on her right. She landed a solid punch on its chest and used the momentum of the strike to twist around and execute a well-aimed kick at the torso of the other Odat. Because she channelled a larger amount of her power into both strikes, the Odats flew into the air as if they had been hit by a speeding car, sending the line of soldiers behind them tumbling like dominoes.

This will have to do, thought Keix, as she jumped to her feet and sprinted after Maii. The mercenaries who had fallen were back on their feet and scrambling over their unconscious comrades. Very soon, they would be on her tail.

Keix pumped her legs harder, reaching Dace at the same time as Maii and Pod. It turned out that Dace hadn't found a room or another corridor for them to go through. Instead, it was the elevator that J had mentioned previously. Just as Keix was about the step into it, someone, or something, gripped one of her ankles and pulled it back. She threw out her hands to break her fall as her lips curled into a snarl. Her foe couldn't be more wrong if it thought that it would be that easy to subdue her. The moment her palms touched the floor, she twisted her body around. Her legs hooked around the Odat's thick neck—if that was what the area where the head and the collar of the uniform met was called—and squeezed. The moment she eased the pressure, her fist flew at the head of the monster. This sent it ploughing across the floor, knocking down several of its advancing colleagues.

Dace slammed his hand onto the button that would close the doors as soon as Keix had got clear of them. The silence rang in Keix's ears, broken only by the heavy breathing of the others.

'Machillian's trying to arrange for a vehicle to get us out of the sector,' Dace said, in reply to the unspoken question hanging in the air. 'J and I managed to override the lift control with this,' he added, jiggling a set of keys that was strung together with an Atros keycard.

Pod stirred. Groaning, he lifted a feeble hand to the spot on his head where he had been clubbed. 'Finally, some fresh air,' he joked in a faint voice.

Maii tsked. 'You're such an idiot,' she reprimanded him.

Dace and Keix were spared acknowledging this exchange when the elevator ground to a halt. But the doors opened just a fraction before they stalled. Cursing, Dace tried scanning the keycard and pushing the button that would open the doors even as the lights overhead flickered.

Forcing her fingers through the small gap between the doors, Keix pried them open. Her initial assumption that the intense light penetrating the slit was from fluorescent bulbs was proven wrong when the first ghost orbs floated in through the solid walls of the elevator. Keix stopped forcing the door open and looked back just in time to see Dace and Maii trying to get a weakened Pod into a corner. A second later, the translucent beings formed an opaque haze surrounding Dace, Maii and Pod.

Blinded by the glow, Keix tried to fend off the phantoms. Stinging pain coursed through her as they brushed against her skin. At the contact, her well of power replenished and she drew on it to keep the agony at bay. She needed to get to her friends and find a way to get them out of this place. They were rendered useless in this fight. Through the haze of the ghosts' assault, she thought she heard screams and anguished whimpers.

Again and again, she channelled her power and swung out her arms wildly. The ghosts were coming at her from every direction, there was no time—nor need—for a strategic fight.

With each strike, the spectres disintegrated before reassembling, weaker than before. Keix did a quick check on her power—it had begun diminishing again. It was then that she realized that only coming into contact with powerful ghosts could recharge her well of power significantly; if the ghosts were weak, there was no point enduring the pain at all. She was drawing power from the ghosts, just like they did from the living.

When she had finally dispersed the thick fog of paranormal energy, she was shocked to see that Maii had conjured up some kind of invisible shield around herself and the flabbergasted Dace and Pod.

'I'll explain later,' said Maii.

If not for their precarious situation, Keix would have demanded that she do so right away. But, as the four of them turned to leave through the doors of the elevator, which were now open, the sight that greeted them left even Keix speechless. Three pairs of yellow eyes were staring unblinkingly in their direction. Flanked by Vin and another dark-haired girl, Seyfer stood facing them.

'Lana?' Dace's apprehensiveness was apparent in his bare whisper.

'I missed you, Dace,' replied the dark-haired girl, but her tone sent an icy shiver down Keix's spine.

Dace seemed mesmerized by the hybrid Lana.

How had Seyfer recovered so quickly? Panic rose in Keix's throat. But there was an even more pressing issue at hand. How on earth was she going to take down three hybrids alone? What was worse, the three monsters had a large contingent of ghosts right behind them. One semi-transparent figure that looked to be leading the ghostly contingent caught her eye.

'Rold,' choked Maii.

Rold's ghost acknowledged her with a smug smile—an expression Keix had never thought she would ever see on the face of the amicable boy that she had gotten to know within a short time.

Perhaps it was the shock of seeing Vin. Oron. Lyndon. And now Rold. Or a combination of all the surprises that had come her way in the past twenty-four hours. But think as she might, Keix couldn't, for the life of her, figure out how they were going to get out of this one.

15

Rebirth

Keix felt Maii's hand slip into hers. Was Maii trying to send her a message? This was as dead an end for her party as she could think of. What would happen next was anyone's guess. Instead of snatching her hand back, which was what her natural instincts told her to do, Keix remained still. It was only with great restraint that she managed to keep a straight face when she felt a little buzz from her palm. The energy traced its way to the back of her skull to join the well of power that Zenchi had unlocked, stimulating its growth. At the same time, Keix felt a warmth growing inside her, chasing away the wariness and fatigue.

'I can see what you're doing, Maii,' said Rold in a threatening voice. At the hybrids' questioning looks, he elaborated, 'She's channelling her Ifarl powers to help Keix replenish her power . . .' he turned to Seyfer with mocking eyes ' . . . the power that allowed her to beat *you*.'

Vin and Lana sniggered at that even as Seyfer let out a low growl. His expression was still menacing and crazy, but there was a touch of cautiousness in his bearing as he sprang at Keix.

With little warning, the battle began in earnest. Maii let go of Keix's hand and stepped back to cast a shield around Pod and Dace, who hadn't recovered from the shock of seeing Lana. Maii's timing proved impeccable. A second after she had moved away, Seyfer tackled Keix onto the floor. She grimaced as she landed on her back. But the brief replenishment of her power that Maii had provided her with had done its job. The energy was flaring brighter beyond Keix's wildest imagination, spreading into and electrifying even the tips of her fingers and toes. Overcome with delirium, she pushed against Seyfer and watched in satisfaction as he flew up and was slammed against the wall.

'Leave the rest alone. We just want Keix,' commanded Vin. At that, the ghost troop rushed Keix. The abrupt and intense light from the orbs and the phantoms blinded her, but she was relieved that her friends would be spared the assault. She flung out punches and kicks in no particular direction, trying to disperse the apparitions. They were clustered so thickly around her that Vin and Lana were nowhere in sight.

But this group of ghosts headed by Rold was different from the ones Keix had encountered before. While those had a singular aim of drawing away the life force of a person, these ones danced around her, like buzzing pests, touching her lightly before flitting away, refusing to engage her in a fight. With each touch, they drained a little of her power. It was insignificant but annoying.

An image of Maii's shield came to Keix's mind and an idea—one that she thought was rather brilliant—struck her.

Rold had just said that the power that Zenchi had unlocked in her was of Ifarl origin. If Maii could project a forcefield to keep the ghosts from reaching her, couldn't Keix do the same to attack the paranormal beings at the same time? After all, Maii's abilities seemed more defensive, while hers were offensive.

Keix nodded to herself in resolution. She drew on the glowing energy and directed it to every part of her skin. She felt her skin heat up, beginning to hum, and almost vibrate with the alien strength coursing through it. It was all or nothing. With a great effort, she pushed this layer of pulsating power outwards, feeling it expand and reach beyond her body in an arc. This sphere pushed the phantoms away from her. Inside this bubble of hers, she heard nothing. A strange calm settled into her as her feet lifted off the ground and a tiny voice within told her to hold on just for a second longer. Keix took in a deep breath. When she exhaled, the air and power surged away from her.

Eyes widening, Keix watched as the sphere that she had created, outlined in a white glow, disintegrate each and every one of the beings in the ghost troop that Vin had set loose on her. The orbs and translucent spectres appeared dull in comparison to her expanding globe. Even though it felt like a lifetime to Keix, it was all over in a split second. With the elimination of the phantoms, Keix could now see Vin and Lana, both rolling on the floor. What surprised her the most, however, was that Rold was still standing. His expression had lost its hostile animation and his eyes, although wide open, were unfocused.

Keix took the chance to glance back at Maii, Dace and Pod. All three of them were gaping at her.

Pod found his voice first. 'That was—' he began, before giving up altogether and settling for a shrug.

'Impressive,' concluded Maii. And for the first time, she looked at Keix like she meant it.

'You're not getting away so easily,' snarled a familiar voice from behind them.

Whipping her head around, Keix saw that it was Vin who had spoken. Her eyes were now a dark yellow, the glow muted. Lana and Seyfer too, were back on their feet. Their cocky demeanours from before had been replaced with pure antagonism.

Beside her, Keix's three friends adopted defensive postures in response to the hybrids dashing towards them. As Vin came face to face with her, Keix's resolve faltered. Not only did she have to come to terms with the fact that she was fighting her best friend—or what was left of her best friend—she had used up all the stored power that supplemented her physical abilities. Her hesitance earned her a sharp kick at the side of her waist. Yet, Keix was shocked to find that it didn't hurt as much as she had expected. Had the force that she had conjured up just now managed to diminish the strength of these inhuman beings?

As if in answer to her question, her peripheral vision showed her Pod flipping Seyfer backwards.

Dace, on the other hand, seemed to be struggling internally like Keix as Lana circled him. He kept backing away from her with a tortured look.

'Keix! Dace! They're not your friends anymore!' shouted Maii from the sidelines.

Why was she was standing beside Rold instead of joining them? wondered Keix.

'Friends,' scoffed Vin as she landed another punch on Keix's shoulder. 'What good are they?'

Jolted back to her senses, Keix finally gathered herself together enough to fight back. She thrust out her fist and caught Vin under the chin. Before Vin could stagger backwards, Keix kneed the side of her hip and pinned her to the wall in one quick move. Vin's struggles ceased when Keix landed a decisive chop to the back of her neck and she dropped to the ground.

Keix turned her attention to Dace, but realized that he, too, had subdued Lana. The girl he had once admired was now an immobile heap at his feet. Dumbfounded, he was looking down at his hands as if he couldn't believe what he had done. The only person who seemed triumphant was Pod. Seyfer had never been an acquaintance, much less a friend, before he had been made a hybrid. And after that, he certainly hadn't presented himself as the frontrunner in a congeniality contest.

'I'm sorry about this, Keix,' said Maii all of a sudden.

Confused, Keix turned to her. 'What?'

'Dace, Pod, hold Keix against the wall,' ordered Maii. This time, Keix recognized the sing-song tone that Maii adopted whenever she went into her Ifarl-command mode.

Keix tried to get away. But Pod and Dace, who were just inches away from her, had jumped to obey Maii's command. Dace's and Pod's shell-shocked faces reflected

Keix's as they gripped her arms and pinned her to the wall, just as she had done to Vin only moments ago. Keix struggled to break free from restraint, only to realize that all her strength had left her. Her muscles now burned with an intensity she had never felt before.

Why was Maii doing this? Anger and panic rose from the centre of her being and closed up Keix's throat. Blood roared through her ears, warming her face.

Maii raised her arms and chanted in a foreign language. Even though Keix couldn't understand the words, she was willing to bet her life that they were the same ones that Zenchi had spoken when unlocking the power within her. Keix's hair stood on end. She let out a gasp as an expressionless Rold floated towards her. Her body began shaking—whether due to Rold's proximity or her rising fury, Keix couldn't tell.

Just when she thought that the anguish from Maii's betrayal couldn't get worse, a burly figure stepped up behind Maii.

'Oron?' asked Pod, shocked. But his hold on Keix didn't loosen.

'Is it done?' Oron asked Maii in his solemn voice.

'Almost,' answered Maii through her teeth. Her lips were drawn tight as she concentrated on executing her spell.

'What's going on, Maii?' asked Dace. Like Pod, his grip on Keix remained tight even as bewilderment surged through him.

Rold's nose was almost touching Keix's. Any power that she had had to resist ghosts was long and well gone.

There was nothing she could do as a single touch from Rold flooded her mind with his last memories, their identities combined into one.

Keix watched as a distorted image of her sitting on the forest floor spoke.

' . . . you're rebel royalty?' she asked, in a high-pitched voice. Indignation rushed through her. *How would she ever understand?* she thought. *They are no different from the humans. Close-minded and useless . . .*

The hut appeared in front of her as she waved her hands to conceal it with an ancient Ifarl spell. *Why do I even bother? Her life's not worth a tenth of mine, no matter what they say about the bigger picture . . .*

A helmeted figure stepped forward and fired at her. At the spot where the dart pierced her skin, agony gushed through her. *This is all Keix's fault. None of this would have ever happened if I hadn't been assigned to babysit her. Why did it have to be me? I will get my revenge . . .*

Resentment pervaded her every pore like an insidious virus, multiplying as it spread. Before long, it was the only thing she could think about. Rold's thoughts left her mind. But his obsession with vengeance had merged with the very essence of her being. The more she thought about how she planned to get back at everyone else in her life—Maii, who had betrayed her, Zej, who had lied to her and joined a rebel group behind her back, Pod and Dace, who just annoyed her, and more—the more serene she felt. Tit for tat. She could almost taste the sweetness of that.

The haze obscuring Keix's vision lifted with this epiphany. Once again, strength surged through her. Unlike the Ifarl power, which was warm and steady, this was icy, giving her a refreshing jolt of energy every now and then. It kept things interesting.

All ready to dole out scathing retorts and to fight back against her captors, Pod and Dace, Keix willed her consciousness back to her body. To her annoyance, she was no longer held against a wall. In fact, she wasn't bound at all. She had been thrown into a cage in the woods. It was night and there was a glow emitting from some distance in front of her cage.

Vin, Lana and Seyfer, for some reason or another, were in the cage with her. They were unconscious. Instead of the animosity and fear she had felt towards them previously, there was a new, fragile thread of affinity that seemed to link them together.

She looked to her right. There was another cage similar to the one she was in. In it, she could see Lyndon and the bodies of the people she had saved from the underground cavern in PEER. An outpouring of hostility overcame her. *If not for these useless people, I would never have been caught. To think that I placed a value on their lives, their well-being,* snarled the voice in her head, in disgust.

The air was acrid, as if someone was burning toxic waste nearby. But as far as Keix could tell, there was no obvious telltale sign that she could use to determine their location—at least not in the clearing where the two cages were held. But surely, if she and her new prison mates worked together, they would find a way out of this. She was just about to rouse them when three figures, one petite and the other two stocky and sturdy, approached the bars of her cage, silhouetted against the orange glow. Keix's irritation grew as she saw who it was. 'Oron. Zenchi. Machillian,' she intoned in the most frigid voice she could muster. *So these three were in cahoots—what with one telling her to trust a friend, another claiming to be a friend and the last pretending to be a saviour.*

Oron spoke first. His tone was solemn, and his eyes were filled with a regretful sadness, 'I'm sorry it had to come to this, Keix.'

But the apology did little to allay Keix's resentment. Instead, the icy anger within her flared. Even though it was apparent that Oron was standing out of her reach, she threw her weight at the bars in a bid to reach him. The steadfast prison didn't even rattle.

'When I get my hands on you, I will make you pay,' threatened Keix with a low growl.

'The cage is fortified with Ifarl magic. You won't get out, unless I let you,' said Zenchi with a benign smile.

While her mellifluous voice was exactly the same as Keix remembered, it now grated on her nerves. 'And *you*,' she added, 'you manipulative hag! I don't give a hoot about your stupid agenda, whatever it is. Let me out. Let me out of here. Right now.'

Zenchi's smile remained but she shook her head. 'Do you not see what has happened to you?' she asked.

Keix let out a cold laugh at Zenchi's words. 'I have been enlightened. That's what has happened. Every single one of you has lied to me. You,' she pointed a finger at Oron, 'told the world you were dead, when you were still secretly working for Atros. The "attack" in Sector L was staged, wasn't it? And you knew all about it.'

Oron shook his head. 'No, I didn't. I only found out about it later on, after my supposed death.'

'Do you think I'd believe anything you say? You two-faced creep!' Keix spat. 'Pretending to be an exemplary Atros soldier—someone beyond reproach—while working secretly with Oka to undermine the organization. And that cryptic message asking me to trust my *friend*—' she scoffed '—you left it after you "died", didn't you?'

'And you—' she pointed the accusing finger at Zenchi '—turning up right after I listened to the message. All of this—staged! And Dace, Pod, Zej, Maii—Maii, oh, I will rip her limb from limb. And I will enjoy every scream that I tear from her throat.'

'Listen to how bloodthirsty you sound,' said Zenchi, shaking her head again. 'That is the trademark of every hybrid.'

The admission from Zenchi caught Keix by surprise, but she didn't let it show on her face. A hybrid? Her heart leapt. She thought back to how strong and fast Seyfer had been the last time they had fought. 'Then you're doomed.' Turning to Machillian, she added, 'You too. A worthless *leader* of an even more worthless rebel group. When the rest of them wake up, we will tear this cage apart and none of you will have anywhere left to run!' Keix allowed herself a laugh at that thought.

'No,' protested Zenchi with little aggression. 'You will be sacrificed tonight to close the portal. I'm sorry I can't save you, Keix. I liked your spirit from the first time I saw you. But, alas, your transformation was already halfway done, same as the rest,' she waved her hands towards

Lyndon's cage. 'Young, precious lives that are going to be lost because of Atros's greed for power. We cannot afford to take the risk of not sacrificing someone who straddles both worlds when we close the portal tonight. Thank you for your help in getting them out. No one else was better equipped to do it except for you and your friends,' she added, pressing both her hands to her chest, as if to convey genuine appreciation.

The gesture only served to stoke Keix's anger. 'Spare me your speeches,' she shouted. 'I have no interest whatsoever in what you're talking about.'

But Zenchi wasn't put off by Keix's tone. Instead, she seemed determined to continue. Considering the fact that she was imprisoned, Keix had little choice but to listen to her ramble on.

'Rold,' Zenchi paused and sighed, 'Poor Rold told you the story behind the Ifarl rhyme, "The Night of Legends".'

Keix didn't deign to answer. All she wanted was for the pests standing in front of her to leave her alone so she could figure out how to get out of here. To make her stand more evident, she turned her back on them and sat down on the floor of the cage.

'This rhyme is but one half of a longer one. The next two verses hint that the problem, if left unsolved for four generations, may be put right by sacrificing the descendent of the one who created the problem in the first place.' Zenchi looked up. 'Tonight is the night.'

Keix gave in to her curiosity and she cast her eyes to the skies. The metal bars that lined the top of her cage hindered little of her view. Through them, she could make out a row of black dots in the sea of midnight blue. The subtle glow from the fire seeping into the heavens reminded her of one of the sunsets she had once watched with Rold.

'Too bad Rold's dead. Unless you think the descendant is me?' said Keix with a snort. She was more confident of her lineage than she was of her chances of getting out of this cage.

'No, you're not a descendent of Iv't,' answered Zenchi without guile. 'Vin is. She's Rold's cousin. And we had to bind Rold's soul to your body, just to be safe. What you are is just collateral damage created by Atros's experiments.'

The thought of being second to someone else riled Keix up. Once again, the cold energy within her inflamed her resentment. She turned around to face Zenchi. 'Ah. So that is why you made use of me to get Vin out—and Lyndon and the rest, who have all been subjects of Atros's experiments—so that you can bring us here to *close your portal*? Why didn't you just send Maii then? Or assemble a group of Ifarls to infiltrate PEER? I'm sure that with your mind-control abilities, you would have caused less of a ruckus than we had.'

'As Ifarls, we are bound by the laws of nature. Most of the time, our skills and abilities cannot be employed to harm any living being. Maii was not able to defeat the hybrids that had already been created. But you could.'

Keix didn't know what to say to that, so she directed her next question at Oron. If it had annoyed her when he spoke just now, she felt even more infuriated that he remained silent, leaving Zenchi to answer all her questions. 'Is that why you got Seyfer to release me when he caught up to me in the forest?' She wasn't surprised to see Oron shaking his head again. To think that she had looked up to him, this defeated person standing in front of her.

'We needed Zenchi to unlock the paranormal power within you. It is somewhat similar to the energy that Ifarls use in their spells. But Seyfer had tracked you down before Zenchi could do it—she had wanted to wait until you had recovered—and it was an extraordinary stroke of luck that he decided to let you go after capturing you in the forest. I had hinted to him that if he did so, there was a good chance that you would lead him to Oka's headquarters,' Oron elaborated. Looking to Machillian, he added, 'Of course, I gave you fair warning once I got wind of the news, which kept the casualties to a minimum.'

Machillian snorted but otherwise remained silent.

Keix ignored him. The Oka leader was a non-issue. The pressing matter at hand was to get out of her cage but seeing as the other hybrids were still knocked out, she decided to question Oron further to see if she could gain any new information. 'So when did you start working with Oka? And aren't you in charge of Seyfer? You're the head of the Acquisitions team, after all, right? Where are we, anyway?'

Oron sighed and seemed to be overcoming some internal struggle. 'I've been with Oka for a long time, since Atros began planning to build a ghost army over a decade ago. In the beginning, I was one of those who thought there might be some merit to the idea. But things just spiralled out of control—at least internally. Atros's citizens had no idea what was going on . . . they don't, even now.

The attack at Sector L two years ago was one of their experiments gone wrong. I had raised concerns about our inability to contain a huge contingent of ghosts like that.'

He paused, and his tone was tight when he continued his explanation. 'I was the one who meddled with the schedules so Zej would run into you at the corridors. And I was the one who sent J to get you guys out at the holding cells. With Seyfer and Vin guarding me'—he gave a bitter smile—'I couldn't say much. But Lana still managed to figure my plan out, so she sounded the alarm and let the guards loose on you.'

Keix stared at Oron. The lines at the corners of his eyes looked deeper and while he used to move with conviction, his attitude was more wary now. How he did expect her to react—with gratitude? Perhaps it would have meant something to her before, but with her newfound detachment, everything just seemed to float past the seething rage within her.

So focused was Keix on this conversation that she failed to notice that five other figures had come up behind Zenchi and Oron.

Turning to them, Oron gave a curt nod before stepping away.

'Say your last goodbyes. We don't know how the ritual will turn out,' said Zenchi in a comforting tone to the rest of them before turning to leave with Oron and Machillian.

Keix cast a look of pure hatred at the five people standing before her.

Zej and Maii's expressions were closed but Pod's distress was written all over his face. Dace appeared defeated as he looked back and forth from Keix to Lana. J, on the other hand, hung back from the group. It was obvious that he wished that he was anywhere but there.

'Keix,' said Pod. 'I know you're still in there somewhere. Is there no way you can fight through this madness?'

Snarling, Keix hissed out her next words. 'Madness? You put me through this. You put me here. *All of you*! But you're wrong. This is not madness. Never in my life have things been clearer for me, traitors!'

'I'm sorry, Keix,' muttered Zej. 'I never expected it to come to this.'

'But that's what you do best, isn't it?' Dace snapped at Zej. 'Sacrifice a few lives for the good of thousands of others.'

'Dace, let me out. And Lana,' Keix pretended to plead. 'We're no different from who we were before.'

Dace stepped forward, his eyes filled with hope. Maii tried to stop him but he brushed her hand away. When he came within reach of Keix, she reached her arms through the cage and grabbed his neck, placing him in a chokehold. The rest of them rushed forward.

'Stay where you are and let me go or he dies,' shouted Keix as Dace spluttered. She kept her grip firm, but not tight enough to cut off Dace's air. It would be stupid to kill the only leverage she had.

'All right, all right,' said Zej in a conciliatory tone. He held out a bunch of keys and jiggled them in Keix's direction. 'Let Dace go and I will unlock the cage.'

'Do you seriously think I'm that stupid?' scoffed Keix.

'Look, the lock is right between you and Dace. I'm not bluffing,' replied Zej, inching closer to them.

Keix relaxed her hold on Dace a little and looked down. Zej was right. There was a little square between her captive and her. 'Throw me the keys, and I will let him go,' she said. Even if the five of them were to rush at her at the same time, Keix was confident that she would be able to take them down.

'Okay,' conceded Zej. He was almost within arm's length of Dace. 'Let go of Dace with one arm and I will pass you the keys, all right?'

Keix did as he requested but she kept her other arm around Dace's neck. At the moment of the exchange, Zej gripped her fingers and twisted them upwards instead of handing the keys over to her. The rest of the gang rushed forward to help pry her arm away from Dace. The cage and their numbers tipped the scales in their favour as they wrested Dace out of her grip. Keix let out a bellow at being tricked again and the icicles of rage surged through her, threatening to rip her apart.

Zenchi's voice cut through her fury. 'It is time,' she said, as a line of people dressed similarly in grey robes surrounded the cages. *Ifarls*, thought Keix. It was the greatest number of this race she had ever seen, and she realized that Vin's pink hair was genetic. Besides the occasional bald-headed Ifarl, the rest of them had varying degrees of pink hair. Maii, who had joined in the procession, looked out of place in her black leather outfit. Zenchi must have been the oldest of the group, with hair as white and bright as the fluorescent lights in PEER.

Zej and the rest helped Dace out of the circle as the Ifarls joined hands to close up the ring. Zenchi tipped her head back and began chanting in that foreign language Keix had heard her use before. Soon, the rest of the robed figures joined in the chant, which now echoed eerily around the clearing. The volume amplified as air whipped around the cages, confined within the circle. But the hems of the Ifarls' robes barely fluttered.

The skies above seemed to darken as the chant increased in intensity and speed, but the nine black dots remained visible.

A hollow silence rang through Keix's ears and the sharp smell of toxic fumes from before intensified and pervaded her nose. White-hot light ignited within her, burning out from the very core of her being. The frosty power that gave her strength and clarity melted in this new inferno that had formed within her. Agony shot through her. The battle between these two forces consumed her until a bright white light was all she could see. It reached a crescendo and stayed there—for how long, Keix didn't know. She didn't need to know. In that moment, she became everything and nothing.

16

New Beginnings

A slender figure watched as the crimson sun made its descent across a violet sky tinged with pinkish-orange clouds. This striking beauty was criss-crossed by a series of lines, both jagged and straight, and of varying thicknesses. Where these tree-trunks met the brown and maroon carpet of fallen leaves, they projected shadows that reached out towards the figure and wound unobtrusively around her like an intangible embrace

Rarely seen, but always heard, the qiues, which called this place home, twittered along. The girl recognized it as their usual song celebrating a day well-spent foraging for their favourite seeds, playing catch with their fellow inhabitants and warbling snatches of song, in search of something new to add to their repertoire.

The refreshing smell of wood and soil soothed her, as did the light breeze. Dried leaves crackled behind her, signalling the approach of someone, but she didn't bother to turn her head. Soon, the infinite beauty of this moment would be lost, never to be relived again.

'Keix,' a voice called out. 'Pod asked me to let you know that dinner's ready.'

'Thanks, Maii,' said Keix.

Three days earlier, Keix had woken up in a rustic bedroom. It had been nothing like the ones she had been in since her escape from PEER. There had been something familiar about it, although she couldn't pinpoint what it was exactly. When she recalled how she had been used as a pawn in this 'bigger picture' that the Ifarls had put her in, she didn't quite know what to feel. Gone was the vengefulness that had raged through her when she had been a hybrid. In its place was a space hollowed out by the pain that she had felt during the Ifarls' ritual—a ritual to close the ghostly portal in a bid to restore their idea of balance to the world.

She had walked out of the room to see the people whom she had viewed as friends, both old and newly made—Zej, Pod, Maii, Dace, Lana and Vin—gathered in the living room of Dace's lake house. Except Lana and Vin, the rest of them had identical, apprehensive expressions as they stared at her.

It seemed impossible to express how she had felt at seeing the people who had been willing to sacrifice her life for a shot at saving the world. She didn't know *what* she was supposed to feel in the first place. So, she plastered on a smile to cover up her confusion and to reassure them that she was glad to still be alive. Keix had come to the conclusion that a hybrid was made when a ghost and a living person fused together—the latter serving to 'house' the resentment and hatred of the former—by Ifarl magic, like what happened with her and Rold as Maii cast the spell.

This would mean that there had been a rogue Ifarl working with Atros to create the hybrids—Seyfer, Vin and Lana—unless Atros had figured out a way to do so on their own. The memory of Zenchi chanting in that strange language on the night the portal was closed flashed through Keix's mind. *Not that it matters anymore, now that the portal is closed*, she reassured herself.

The closure of the portal had ripped away all traces of paranormality from this dimension, including the souls of the dead that had been bonded to the four of them—Keix, Vin, Lana and Seyfer. And they had reverted to their old selves. Physically, at least.

The loss of Rold hung thick in the air. Seeing his ghost was confirmation that he had died from the allergic reaction to the sedative. But closing the portal added a sense of finality to his death.

Keix extracted herself from her thoughts and proceeded to walk back to the lake house. But Maii's voice stopped her.

'He's sorry, you know? We both are.'

Keix didn't need to ask to know that the 'he' Maii was referring to was Zej. She thought for a long moment. 'There's nothing to be sorry for.'

'I've seen the way he looks at you when your attention is elsewhere,' continued Maii.

Keix coughed to cover up her surprise. Maii was the last person she had ever thought would give her relationship advice.

'I think you're overthinking it,' said Keix. Her clipped tone indicated that she didn't want to discuss the matter further, and she was surprised when Maii acceded to her unspoken wish with a nod.

The two of them entered the house together before Maii disappeared down one of the hallways.

Keix was still getting used to the changes in the sitting area. What used to be a dusty and deserted space had regained its character bit by bit with the care the group had showered on it in the past week. Colourful throw pillows that reminded Keix a little of the Sector L sitting area adorned the luxurious leather sofa.

Zej was sitting on this, with his head bowed, as if in deep thought.

The delicious smell of roasted chicken floated in through the archway that connected the sitting area to the kitchen. Keix grabbed a drink and tried to slink into the corner furthest from Zej. From her new spot, she could see the mantelpiece clearly. This fixture too, had been wiped down, and a cosy fire danced in the space below it.

Before long, Vin caught her eye and walked towards her.

In her best friend's eyes, Keix recognized a haunted look that reflected her own. She wondered if it would ever go away. Like Keix, Vin seemed to have lost her carefree spirit. 'Some celebration, huh,' said Vin.

Keix shrugged and smiled. 'Well, it's not like you don't know Pod.'

Both of them fell silent at that. The chasm that separated them from their past selves felt like a black hole that would never ever close up.

'Where do you think Seyfer went?' asked Keix. She no longer shuddered at her memory of Seyfer. After all, she had behaved the same way when she had been transitioned too. She wondered what he was truly like. But she had not got the chance to find out, since he had left them without a word as soon as he had woken up.

Vin shrugged in answer. 'I never really knew him, I guess.'

Pod's voice interrupted their stiff conversation. 'Hey, Keix and Vin! Stop sulking in the corner. Dinner's ready.'

Everyone filed into the kitchen at his request. Since Keix was the last one through the door, she had to take the only seat left, which was at the head of the table, with Maii and Zej on either side.

Beside Maii, Pod was talking about his latest foray into the Atros sector, ' . . . things look unchanged on the outside, but the guards at the sector border have dwindled in numbers and quality. I could have strolled past the checkpoint and no one would have guessed that I'm an Atros soldier gone AWOL,' he said with a laugh. 'And people have no idea that their biggest threat has been eliminated! No one knows that the ghost portal has been closed. It's business as usual, which is kind of weird, yet not unexpected.'

A question that she wanted to ask Maii suddenly crossed Keix's mind, and she almost kicked herself for not bringing it up when they had been alone just now. But, since everyone else was listening to Pod, she figured there was no harm in doing so now. Keix turned to her. 'Maii,' she whispered. 'Before Zenchi and you guys closed the portal, she said something about "The Night of Legends" being one half of a rhyme. Do you know the other half?'

'Why do you want to know?'

There was no hostility in Maii's tone, which Keix took as an encouraging sign. So she decided to come clean with her intentions. 'I . . . I don't know. But I think it might help me make sense of what happened—what I felt—during the ritual,' she confessed.

Maii's eyes softened but she hesitated for a moment. Perhaps she felt like she owed Keix an explanation for manipulating her. Maii drew her lips tight before she said, 'The poem's called "Act of Repentance".'

The mellifluous way in which she recited the poem reminded Keix of Rold again, and she felt a pang of guilt. But she listened intently to Maii's words, memorizing them.

Stars of nine,
Forgo shine,
Line the skies,
Break the ties.
Condemn,
Repent,
Bae we renounce in assent.

Failure stains,
Power wanes.

Deadly dance,
Single chance.
Chant right,
Tread light.
Plunge anew into the night.

An uneasy feeling crept through Keix. Zenchi had said that this second half of the rhyme suggested that Iv't's actions 'may be put right by sacrificing the descendent of the one who created the problem in the first place'. And it sounded to Keix that the Ifarls had only one shot at righting Iv't's wrongs—still, she couldn't be sure. Unlike Rold, Maii didn't bother to explain the cryptic words.

Throughout the rest of dinner, Keix smiled and responded to the ebb and flow of the conversation in whatever way she felt was appropriate. She was still hung up on the poem when she retired to her room, so she wrote down the words and read through them again and again.

Keix jumped when a knock sounded at her door.

'Who's that?' she asked, wondering who would want to talk to her at this late hour. Pod's raucous laughter had died down a long while ago and the entire household had wound down for the night after that.

A familiar but hesitant voice came through the door. 'It's me, Zej. Can I come in?'

Keix opened the door just enough for him to slip in before shutting it again.

'Am I interrupting something?' asked Zej, gesturing to the slip of paper in Keix's hands.

Hastily, Keix folded it into a small rectangle and tucked it into the pocket of her jeans. 'No, I was just . . .' she trailed off without further explanation. 'Do you want to sit down?' She pointed to the single armchair in the corner.

Shaking his head, Zej remained standing at the door facing Keix. An awkward silence fell. Keix looked around the room and considered whether she should sit back down on the bed or continue standing. But Zej spoke before she came to a decision.

'I'm sorry, Keix,' he said. 'For letting the Ifarls go on with the ritual.'

'Huh?' Keix responded without letting the implications of Zej's words sink in first.

'I let Zenchi go ahead with the ritual even though I knew it might kill you.' A tortured expression crossed Zej's narrowed eyes. 'I should have fought harder for you, like Dace did.'

'Dace? Well, he wasn't actually fighting for me,' Keix shrugged. When Zej didn't reply, she attempted to lighten the mood, 'and he didn't exactly put up a very good fight, did he?' she said with a laugh. 'I still managed to get him into a chokehold. I mean, not me, but the hybrid me.'

'I know that there's no point saying this now—justifying our actions—but you should know that none of us knew Zenchi's endgame. She kept mum about the "sacrifice" part until we had you guys in cages. No one realized that she was just using everyone. Pod, Dace, and even Machillian. Maii was the only person who was in the know. I'd never seen Pod so angry and confused. After Maii forced your transition, the Ifarls did the same to Lyndon and the rest of the people we rescued from PEER. The Ifarls said that all of you had to be transitioned fully in order for the ritual to work. We, even Oron, thought we were keeping you guys imprisoned for your safety.'

Keix didn't know what to say to that. She tried to recall if there was any awkwardness between Pod and Maii, but she realized she couldn't tell because she had not been paying attention to everything going on around her since that fateful night.

A long silence fell. Keix wondered whether Zej was looking for forgiveness or reassurance. 'It was the right thing to do,' she said finally.

'Was it? I thought it was the right thing to do. To obey Oka's orders to send Lana to her doom too. Dace didn't. That's why he behaves the way he does towards me. It's because when—'

'I know what happened with Lana. Dace told me.'

'He did?'

Keix nodded.

'I'm a coward.' Zej's bitterness was written all over his face.

Sighing, Keix weighed her next words. 'You're not. You just placed too much faith in Atros—and Oka. Both of them had their own agendas. The Ifarls too. And sometimes, their motives don't line up with ours. But you can stop beating yourself up. I would have done the same if I were in your shoes.' As the words left her lips, Keix realized that she had come to terms with her friends' decision to go through with the ritual a long time ago.

'Will you ever forgive me?' asked Zej, still uncertain.

Nodding her head, Keix couldn't stop herself from blurting out, 'Have you spoken to Lana about this?'

'Lana?' Zej's look of relief turned to one of confusion. 'What has Lana got to do with this?'

'Well, you were ready to sacrifice her. And Vin too,' Keix pointed out.

Guilt flashed in Zej's eyes before it was replaced with embarrassment. 'Yes, I owe them apologies too. I just . . . wanted to talk to the most important person first.'

Keix recalled Maii's words from earlier and felt her face heating up.

'I like you, Keix. I've liked you since ATI but I just enjoyed our status quo too much to want to jeopardize our friendship. And after Sector L and PEER . . . and that night of the ritual . . . I just wish I had done something different, somewhere.'

Keix swallowed, taken aback by Zej's confession. He had taken a step forward and was standing as close to her as the time they hid in the tiny closet in the abandoned building from Atros soldiers. This time, however, he smelled of his minty aftershave with the lingering scent of herbs and beer from the meal they had shared, instead of sweat, blood and garbage. The moonlight streaming in through the sheer curtains, coupled with the cosy orange glow from the bedside lamps made his eyes look like molten metal. Any ambient sound that was present was drowned out by the rapid beating of her heart.

Zej had laid his cards on the table. *Can we come back from this?* Keix asked herself. *Do I want to?*

Keix got her answer when her head tilted up to meet Zej's. A jolt ran through her when their lips touched. Encircling her in his arms, he pulled her closer. She reached her hands up and rested them on his shoulders, letting the heat from his neck warm her cold fingers.

When they finally broke apart, Zej held on to Keix as their hearts raced in tandem, having crossed an invisible threshold. Except for another peck that he planted on her forehead before leaving the room, no other words were exchanged between them.

Keix was still standing on the spot where she had kissed Zej when Dace knocked on her door. The sudden sound pulled her back to the present.

'Hey,' said Dace.

'Hey, yourself,' returned Keix. Her emotions were still in turmoil but part of her was glad to see Dace. They hadn't spoken much since she had woken up, and he had looked as preoccupied and haunted as Vin, Lana and herself.

'I saw Zej slip out of your room.' The statement was meant to be teasing, yet there was little humour in his tone.

'Hmm.' Keix shrugged. She searched for another topic and asked the first question that came to her mind. 'How are things between you and Lana?'

Dace's eyes darkened in torment. 'Things are . . . different.'

Both of them fell quiet for a long while.

'Well, I guess it's hard not to change. I mean, she's been through a lot,' reasoned Dace. He paused before adding, 'You've been through a lot.'

'That's kind of an understatement,' said Keix with a genuine smile.

Dace returned one of his own. He reached out to take Keix's hand and clasped it between his palms. His hands felt surprisingly warm against hers as a sense of peace settled between them. After a long time, he patted her hand and said, 'I'm glad I met you, Keix.'

Keix watched the door close behind Dace, wondering why their conversation had left knots in her stomach. Reflexively, she reached up to touch the charm of the necklace that was supposed to be an heirloom from her Kulcan father. The sensation brought forward the memory of the moments after the ritual had concluded.

Still numb from the pain of the ritual, she had woken up to a burning sensation in the hollow of her throat where her necklace's stone charm sat. The sun had been peeking over the horizon and the gentle rays illuminated the repercussions of the pandemonium from moments ago. The Ifarls, still holding hands, had all fallen onto their backs at the impact of the spell they had cast. In a jagged circle, they enclosed the two cages they had surrounded. Everyone was unconscious, from the hybrids in her cage to Pod, Zej, Dace and J, who were outside the circle.

In her delirious state, Keix had seen a figure coming towards her. It was a man riding an animal she had never thought she would see in her life—a shih. The rider slowed as he drew nearer to her. He reached behind him and pulled out the broadsword that was strapped to his back. In one swift movement, he brought the weapon down on the cage's lock and split it apart. Then, he had looked straight into Keix's eyes and said something to her.

Keix had thought that he must be an illusion created by her addled mind, but the words the Kulcan had said were seared as distinctly into her memory as the letter that had come with her necklace all those years ago.

Bringing her thoughts back to the present with a resolute nod, Keix slipped out of the room, away from the lake house and into the freedom of the woods. She had a mission to undertake—but whether it was real, or merely a figment of her imagination, there was only one way to find out. She was going to have to find her Kulcan father.

END

Acknowledgements

My sincerest and deepest thanks to Nora Nazarene, without whom the publication of this novel would not have been possible. Thank you for replying to my random LinkedIn message, accepting my unsolicited manuscript submission, reading it, and liking it enough to take a chance on this story.

I would also like to thank the National Arts Council for investing in the literary scene in Singapore and initiating the Mentor Access Project. It was through this programme that I met Dave Chua, my mentor, who has an uncanny way of giving sage advice without ever intruding on my voice. The first draft of this novel wouldn't even had come into existence if not for them, and a lucky combination of events.

To my fellow MAP mentees: Joelyn Alexandra, Agnes Chew, Mickey Lin, Kane Wheatley-Holder, Melissa De Silva, Vicky Chong and Joanna Leng. Thank you guys for being my inspiration even after the year-long programme ended.

To Amanda Yee, my ex-colleague who told me something along the lines that "some authors are talented, but there are others who become authors through hard work", when I expressed my doubts about achieving my dream of becoming a novelist. Yes, I don't remember your exact words, but the gist of the message is what continues to spur me on—so, thank you.

To Corinne Ng, my colleague-turned-friend. I see you as the first spark that got everything going. If you hadn't gotten a job at the Singapore Writers Festival and introduced me to the world of SingLit, it's likely that none of this would have happened. Thank you.

To my friends and family who have been nothing short of encouraging when I started telling you all that I'm writing fiction (for real). Thank you for being interested in my stories and always asking me questions such as, "What's your book about?", "What's happening with your book now?" and cheering with me when I said that my book was going to get published. Your enthusiasm never failed to give me warm, fuzzy feelings. I love you. All of you. Thank you.

Aries, you got the songbird reference here. TY, I've yet to create something quite like you—let's wait and see what comes up next.

To my sister: You get a shout-out only because I've known you for your entire life. You still haven't got back to me about which ending I should go for—and look, now the book's published.

To our dad: Well, I did it despite everything you said.

To my Baby G: I wouldn't have completed the first draft of the book if I hadn't got pregnant with you. I know you don't remember, but you were inside me when I was tapping away at the keyboard for 15 hours a day, and when I did my first public reading at SWF in 2015. To my G Shock: I wouldn't have had the time to revise my manuscript if not for the maternity leave I was taking after giving birth to you. I love both of you so much. And to Hatch, my darling: I know you can't read because you're a dog, but I still want to pen down my thanks to you for being my emotional support and sunshine through the darkest times of my life. I love you, darling.

Lastly, to my husband. I don't know if this is a thanks, per se. But . . . I guess your reverse psychology worked? I know you weren't being mean when you asked me, "How do you know if you are writer material? You may try your entire life and still not succeed in writing a book or getting it published." My reply then was a whole lot of indignation, and I said that I was going to take all the money I made off the book, change it into 1-cent coins and throw it at you—but of course, I'm not going to do that. Now, I will just say, HA. Look who's got the last laugh now. (All right, I still love you.)